MARRIED TO THE MOB

BIANCHI CRIME FAMILY

C.M. STEELE

THE STEELE PRESS

ISBN: 978-1-954645-06-6

❀ Created with Vellum

Married to the Mob

Fascinated. One look and I'd known at that moment that she'd be my wife. Nothing and no one will keep my queen from me, even if I have to wait years to finally claim her. There are no words to express what I'm willing to do to protect our future together.

Aria Grasso is mine.

An arranged marriage. I had no idea that I'd be forced to marry a man I didn't know. I should push him away, but the moment Domani Bianchi and I speak for the first time, I'm confident that it's a lost cause. Domani has decided I'm his, and my body agrees. Not everyone agrees with our upcoming wedding. However, Domani will have his way.

I will be his.

PROLOGUE

Three years earlier

Aria

THE VEHICLE PULLS off the expressway as we head toward O'Hare International Airport, but I can't shake the overwhelming, raw emotion that flows through me. I've just gotten my first up-close look at Domani Bianchi. Granted, he never saw my face the entire time his father and mine spoke. I stare out the window as if somehow I'll still be able to see his brooding handsome face again. It was twenty minutes ago, and I can't stop thinking of him.

"Aria, are you well?" I dart my eyes to my father, wondering if he knows what's going through my head right now. I sure as hell hope not, but the man doesn't give anything away.

I calmly take a breath and say, "Yes, Papa. I'm fine."

"Your face is flush. Are you sure you're alright?"

"I am. I've never been to Ireland. I think I'm getting anxious, nervous or something."

"Couldn't have anything to do with running into Domani Bianchi? He's not going to hurt you no matter how dark his reputation is." *That perceptive man.*

Huffing and fixing the hem of my skirt, I blurt out in a rush, "I didn't actually see him. Anyway. How long until we're there? I want to take a nap." My denial is a little too blatantly obvious, but I hope he drops the subject. Talking about boys with my dad isn't something I care for and I'm sure neither does he, although Domani Bianchi's anything but a boy.

"It's a long flight, so just relax. We'll be boarding soon."

"I can't believe Gloria's getting married," my mother says, tearing up.

"I told you we shouldn't have let her go abroad," my father snarls at my mother, handing her his handkerchief. My sister was supposed to take a semester in England and somehow ended up in Ireland where she met Cormack Delaney.

They're getting married in two days because the man is insanely determined and doesn't care if she ever comes back to Chicago. My father and him had a very long and loud discussion. All things said and done, they're getting married, and we at least get to see it.

We board the plane and I take a nice built small bed and go to sleep. All the while dreams of Domani keep me from wanting to wake up.

I can't wait to get out of here. I thought when we flew over the Emerald Isle that I'd found paradise, but then Peter Delaney appeared out of thin air, sending chills up and down my skin. His eyes linger over me when he believes no one is looking, but I can feel them as if I rushed into a spider's web. The creepy feeling has made my brief stay a nightmare.

"It's time to get ready for the wedding," my mother says, shaking me out of my terrible thoughts. Unfortunately, Peter's standing up at the wedding and we're walking together. His wife is here as well, a pretty lady who appears kind but there's something behind her eyes that is unsettling. Does she fear her husband? Will Cormack be that way with Gloria?

No. I had my answer the second I met my future brother-in-law. He's a great guy and wants to worship my sister to the point that I'm a tad bit jealous. I'd hadn't given marriage that kind of thought until we spotted Domani. Now, it's all my brain can think of. I blame it on the wedding and all the lovey-dovey emotions flying through the air.

It's a little sad because Cormack's father just died a day before Gloria met her fiancé. Still, the day is perfect for the lovely couple. I'll bite down on my own bile and celebrate my sister's happiness and avoid Peter as much as I can.

"It's time, lasses," Peter utters, rapping his knuckles on the door.

"We're ready." I spin around and see my sister in her gorgeous gown, floored by her beauty. My sister is breathtaking and I'm sure Cormack's going to lose it when he sees her perfection.

"Excuse me," I hear my father say behind the door. "I'm coming in." My dad steps into the room, looking handsome as ever in his tux, and his mouth falls open as he stares at Gloria.

"Gloria, you look like an angel."

"Thank you, Papa." He hugs her tightly until she lets out a grunt. I snap a picture on my phone of my sister as she smiles at my dad because this is a painting worthy image.

We leave Gloria's dressing room inside a large Catholic Church only to see Peter waiting for us.

"You should be standing by your brother right now," my father informs Peter.

With a slight frown, he does just that, allowing me a sigh of relief. I hope after today, it's the last I see of Peter Delaney.

PROLOGUE

A year later...

Domani

THE MEETING'S off to a shitty start. I'm ready to shoot the Denali head for questioning my status at the table, but I will not disrespect our host, Don Anthony Grasso, the head of the Grasso Family. I'm representing the Bianchi family on behalf of my father who is, at present, celebrating his anniversary with my mother. Family always comes first to him and it's something he's passed along to his boys.

"We need to calm down and talk territories," Don Grasso says. I'm ready to go to war, but that's not in the best interest of anyone at the moment. Keeping my eyes on Denali, I don't trust that fucker. If he crosses me, I'll treat him to a trip to hell after taking his empire.

"Nothing should fucking change," Diamanté family head exclaims, pounding his fist. His family is losing more and more business and he doesn't want to risk losing it all.

"Listen. We're trying to keep the fucking peace here, gentlemen. I'm talking about the latest infringement we've had in the Grasso and Bianchi areas by both of you."

"I told you mine was accidental." It had been. A stupid dealer looking to make a big score came to our side and started slanging some crack and meth. Both the Grasso and Bianchi families don't deal in drugs because it makes people less willing to pay us our money on time. We tend to work on the books. You want to gamble or need a loan we operate that way. I've only returned from a summer in Italy, learning my roots when my father mentioned retiring. For the past month, I've been learning, so today is my first big meeting with these men. I have to remain strong and yet levelheaded and not the young punk they think I am.

"And ours, the fucking city changed zoning, forcing a block further north."

"Again, we just want to come to an agreement. Keep the fucking dope on your side of the street. Taking cuts isn't something any of us want."

A knock at the door sends Don Grasso's hand up to silence us. "Come in."

A waitstaff comes in to serve us some coffee. The door's ajar as they go around the table, serving us. I don't trust open doors like that, so I watch for any blitz move. I've learned a lot from our homeland counterparts. I'm just about to tell the lady to stop pouring me coffee when something catches my attention out the corner of my eye.

Not *a something*, but rather, *a someone*.

She freezes as our eyes meet. I wonder if she's curious or if she is interested. Who the hell is she? Did Don Grasso intentionally sneak in honey traps, or is she a part of the household staff? I look at her clothes and know it's not the case at all. The raven-haired beauty is in a skin-tight black cocktail dress that reveals a little too much leg for all these men for my liking. Her long black hair lays over her shoulder, adding a level of allure to her already enchanting presence.

My dick stiffens under the table as she stares directly into my soul, making me question my sanity. No one in their right mind can fall that fast. I pull my attention away from her ruby red lips parted so prettily and send my gaze up and down her form. Fuck, her tits are practically popping out of the dress that fits her too snugly. She presses her palm to her hip, almost posing for me and revealing a little more skin with that subtle move. I bite back a growl, wanting to scold her and wrap her up in my coat, so no one else can see her sexy figure.

Getting too carried away, I return my attention to her face and her not so subtle makeup. It's not overdone, just well done and so alluring. I want to bite down on those cherry lips as she whimpers my name. Everything about her calls to me, and I know in that instant that I will make her mine. Never in my life has a beauty like her captivated me enough to forget business. I'd forgotten all the reasons why I'm in the house of one of my rivals, dealing with all my rivals.

The servers leave, closing the door behind them, stealing my queen from my sight. A low growl exits my chest, hating whoever stole her beauty from my presence. I have to know who she is, and I will find out.

"Gentlemen, you must forgive me. I must have a word with the young Mr. Bianchi." I cock my brow up at him and realize that he'd been staring at me the entire time. Shit. Maybe from the look on his face, she's not a honeytrap. Please don't tell me she's his daughter.

"Let's do this." I stand without fear and am grateful that

my hard-on is covered by my suit jacket. I'd hate to make a fool of myself in front of these pussies that I could easily take out.

His guards and mine follow us out of the room and to his study, tensions high.

As soon as we're inside, he turns our men and says, "None of you will be needed. This is a private conversation." He sends his men first, so I nod to mine to follow suit. My cousin, Nero, hesitates and gives me a look to see if I'm sure, and I am, so I nod again. He takes his leave, closing the wooden door behind him.

He runs his fingers through his salt and pepper hair before he presses his finger into my chest. "I'm gonna be frank about this. She's too fucking young for you."

"What? Who?" I question, knowing he has to be talking about my future wife.

He tilts his head down, trying to keep his temper even, but when his eyes meet mine, there's a look of understanding and concern. "Don't play games with me. You were staring at my daughter like you'd found your soulmate or something."

My mouth drops open. It's not what I could have hoped for. She's already taken. "Daughter? I thought your daughter was married." I remember he and his wife were headed to the airport a few years ago.

"Yes, my eldest Gloria is married. Aria is the younger of the two." Aria? What a beautiful name.

"When you say young...how young?" I need to know how fucking sick I am.

"Sixteen."

"Son of a bitch. Sixteen." Damn it. She's not even legal.

"Yes. She's a decade younger than you. I don't know what your intentions are or anything, but she's my little princess.

So, even though we break laws for a living, it's not one I'm willing to let *anyone* cross." He's right about her being too young for me; that's for sure.

Can I wait for her to grow up? I know the answer before I finish the thought.

"I'll wait for her," I insist. There's no doubt in my mind about it.

"Wait for her?" He sits on the edge of his desk, crossing his arms. I don't know if he's trying to create an imposing presence or just taking in what I'm saying, but the man isn't gonna scare me away.

"Yes. You didn't say she couldn't marry me." It's a huge difference that I was quick to pick up on and will use to my advantage.

"You're saying you want to marry my daughter?" he reiterates as if I can be any clearer on the matter.

"That's exactly what I'm saying. You didn't say I didn't deserve her; you said she was too young. In two years' time, she'll be legal in every fucking state in this country, and then she'll be my wife," I inform him because I'm not the kind to back off my word.

It takes him maybe thirty seconds before he sighs and stands. "Here are the rules, and I want you to understand that under no uncertain terms are they to be broken." He tips his head and stares at me with his brows scrunched waiting for me to agree to hear them out.

I nod and cross my arms. "Okay. Let's hear them."

Clearing his throat he says, "One, you don't speak to her at all. I want her to grow up without the pressure of a pending marriage. Two, you don't fuck around on my little girl. If you can't keep it in your pants for the next two years, then the deal's off. I'm not giving my blessing to a piece of shit looking for a piece of property." I nod as he speaks because the first one is for the best, even I can see that, and the second wasn't even a thought in my head.

"Is that it?" I ask.

"You act like that's not enough."

"I have conditions as well. The first one you tossed out is difficult. Still, the temptation will be too great to ignore, so I will easily adhere to it, but that doesn't mean I can't see her from a distance. I'll keep an eye on her always. That's my condition to the first one."

"And the second one?" His brow lifts on that one like he believes that's a deal breaker. Not in my case, so if that's what he had in mind, he picked the wrong guy to try that request on.

"The second's easy. I'm still a virgin. It's not something I'd like everyone to know, but we have standards in my family, and dicking hoes is against the rules. And my father believes any woman that's not my wife doesn't belong in my bed."

"Those are good rules to live by. Still, you do realize that we don't need to speak on this until she's older. Maybe in a couple of years when you've had time to decide if she's the woman for you."

My fists clench at my side at the insult to both me and his daughter. I felt the connection with just a look. "No. I'm set on it. There is no way around it. Aria will be my wife one day. I knew the second she looked at me that she'd be the one."

"Wow, you Bianchi men don't play games. Your father is missing this important meeting for his anniversary, and now you're swearing to wait to marry my daughter."

"Women make the world go round." I'm thinking about the day I can make his daughter round in the belly. Fuck, I shouldn't be thinking about her that way, knowing she's technically a minor and he's standing right in front of me. Besides, I'm a fucking criminal, and she doesn't look like a damn teenager so it shouldn't matter, but I'll wait for my queen to finish growing up.

"Smart man."

"Just so we're clear—I have your blessing?" I'm not leaving here without that reassurance. I don't hedge bets. I follow through with everything, making sure there's no fucking hiccups.

"You do, and will, if you hold up your end."

"Good, then. I will make it clear to all of the families that Aria Grasso is my wife, and no deal or arrangement will be made to stop it or we'll go to war."

"You are one determined man," he chuckles. We shake hands, sealing our verbal contract.

"I know what I want, and I seize it."

"Very well. Let us join the rest of the men."

We exit his study and walk back to the meeting room with our men following behind us. I refuse to look for my bride, making sure to hold up my end of the bargain. Tomorrow, I'll make sure eyes are on her at all times, reporting back to me when I can't observe her myself.

As we enter the room, Don Grasso takes his seat at the head of the table and says, "Mr. Bianchi would like to make a statement."

I nod and clear my throat. "I'm going to be very clear, so there's no mistaking me or the words coming out of my mouth. Aria Grasso will be my wife in two years' time. There will be no offers for her hand by anyone in any family. No deals, no sneaking in to try to take my queen. I am clear?"

They all sit around the table, awed into silence. As my father's second-in-command, I'm filling in for him today and am not the Don just yet, but I refuse to be looked on as weak by any of these men. "Well, gentleman, do we have an understanding?"

"Two years? You might change your mind by then."

"You will learn that I don't change my mind on anything. I've been given Don Grasso's blessing under the guise that she remains unaware of the attachment. So, should anyone speak of it before it's time, I will cut your tongue out personally. Do we understand each other, gentleman?"

A round of nods and agreements goes around the room, earning me a smile from Grasso himself. We continue the meeting without another interruption. Keeping the peace and keeping the cops out of our hair is the biggest priority for our families, so we do our best not to step on each other's toes.

As I take my leave, I steel myself for walking away from my queen, but it's a must. Tomorrow, I will take in her beauty even from a distance.

1

Domani

Present Day

Today's the big day. A text on my phone tells me what I already know, Aria's pissed. They've just broken the news to my queen that she's marrying me. Distant stomping can be heard as she runs up to her room and slams the door. "Fucking asshole. I can't believe it. Ugh," she hisses to the sky. She flops down on her bed, screaming into her pillow. I watch her from my computer for the next thirty minutes, listening to the birthday girl's rage all the while waiting for her to notice her birthday present on her dresser. The one I picked out myself. She rolls onto her side, spotting the box. Snatching it as she sits up in her bed, she opens the envelope and reads the card.

"To my queen,

I wish you a very happy birthday. The last one we will ever spend apart. -Domani"

"Pretty penmanship," she remarks, setting it aside. Tugging on the red ribbon, she frees it and then opens the box. Inside is a bracelet with several charms, including a painter's palette. A gasp and a squeal pass her lips briefly before she looks to the door and then back at the bracelet.

"Nice, but he can't buy me," she huffs, tossing it carelessly into the box and then onto her dresser. She can be upset, but I know in her heart she loves the gift. I've learned everything I could from my queen from a distance. Her love of painting being one of many interesting pieces that make up Aria Grasso, soon to be Aria Bianchi.

Anger from her slips away as she sits there and stews. Once again she picks up the piece and walks over to the trash. I think she's gonna toss it which will get her ass reddened. It's one thing if she didn't like it, but she's doing it to spite me. She drops the box in the bin, but quickly changes her mind and scoops it out. "He's lucky I love it," she mutters as she heads into her bathroom.

I hear the shower turn on, and I jump up to lock my office door. Damn she's got me by the balls. I whip my cock out of my slacks, stroking the already semi-hard shaft. The sound of the water running stiffens my length even further, visualizing my future wife, my queen, naked. It's only been two weeks since I had the cameras put in. Beating my meat, I bust my load quickly, swiping off the sticky mess with a pair of Aria's panties that I confiscated from her room the day I set up the cameras.

I'm not a total sick fuck because I only did it the two weeks before she turned eighteen. Still, I never put one in her bathroom, although the listening device is activated next to the bathroom door for safety precautions. The thought of her falling and slipping has crossed my mind on more than one occasion. It's fucking stupid how obsessed I am with her well-being. I'm about to tuck my dick back inside my trousers when the sounds change.

Moans come from her, catching me by surprise, getting

me hard all over again. Immediately I call John, the guard who keeps watch outside her door. "Get the hell away from her door. I'll tell you when you can come back," I snarl, teeth gnashing as I give my order.

"Yes, sir."

I end the call and return all my attention to Aria and the little performance she's giving me. Damn, it's music to my ears that goes on for a few minutes, but then suddenly stops with a frustrated sigh. She turns off the water and then exits the bathroom wrapped up in a fluffy white towel that covers her from her perfect tits down to the middle of her thighs.

My queen can't get herself off. I wonder if this is a new thing or if she's been strumming her kitty often. I watch the way she moves as she finds the clothes she's going to wear, tension visible in her shoulders.

A knock at the door causes her to jump. "What is it?"

"Sweetie, we're going dress shopping in an hour," she says through the door.

Swinging the door open in nothing but a towel is going to get her in a world of trouble. "This isn't how I want to spend my birthday, mama."

"It will be fine," Signora Grasso says, nudging Aria back into the room before closing the door.

She walks to the dresser and drops her fucking towel, giving me her back and that juicy ass I want to redden and bite into. "Whatever. It's not like I get a choice in anything. Fucking medieval family." I watch her slide on a pair of lace black and red panties with little cherries on them. I'm about to come from the view, but I control the animalistic need to focus on my bride-to-be.

"Watch your mouth young lady. Besides, I'm sure you'll find Domani to be an excellent husband." *Thank you, Signora Grasso.*

"I have to get dressed. How much time do I have?" she asks, turning slightly with her hands on her hips, tits bouncing nicely from this side view.

"Twenty minutes. I'm glad you already showered." Her mother walks back out of the room and Aria slams the door, clearly pissed about the arrangement, so she slips on the tiniest dress she can find, knowing that she's going to attract attention when she goes out to try on wedding dresses. She's lucky she put on a bra before I find myself interrupting their shopping trip. Still, I'm about to snap and break some faces today, it seems. When I look at the dress again, it looks like the one she wore the day I first noticed her. Could it be? Does she know it?

I follow, and my men take note of every fuck who gets out of line. Luckily, only two find their asses beaten with a warning to keep their eyes to themselves or lose their lives. Still, I keep my distance because it's bad luck to see my queen in her wedding gown, and I get a charge for a two-thousand-dollar gown at the shop, so I know she bought one. That eases my mind.

---

*I*t's finally the day of our first meeting. My queen will be mine in just two days. The wait is nearly at an end, and every hour that lingers between us feels like an eternity. I've kept my cool and kept my distance with good reason these past two weeks when I could have introduced myself to my bride. The pent-up lust, the craving to make her mine, would be impossible to fight. Instead, I sit quietly and watch as my queen packs up her room. I see her favorite things, learn more and more about her through these stolen moments. It's sick and cruel to invade her space like this, but I've been hanging on by a thread.

A knock on my office door distracts me from my queen for just a moment. "Yes?"

"I need a minute with you, Domani."

"Come in, Mama." She barrels in before I get the words completely out, her hair still in a towel but her dress on.

"What are you doing sitting around here? She's coming soon, and you can't be looking a mess. She's wearing a red dress tonight, so find something to match." Mothers. I have a feeling she was going to get a bit insane as the wedding gets closer. I'm the one who should be freaking the fuck out, but then again, I just busted a nut, so I've calmed my ass down.

"I will," I tell her.

She doesn't know that I've already seen the garment and have my suit ready and waiting for me. "I have a few more hours before they are scheduled to arrive. Although, I'll have you know that I'm going to pick her up myself, so I'll be getting ready soon. I promise that I won't disappoint my queen. I've been waiting for this day for a long time."

"Good. I'd leave the scruff unless you're planning to get her alone," she says with a wink before walking out of my office and closing the door behind her.

"Then a shave is a must," I growl to myself. I might not fuck her tonight, but that doesn't mean I won't try to eat her pussy for dessert or as an appetizer. The thought of spreading her out and thrusting my tongue into her wet slit makes me hard again.

I take a deep breath and think of anything else to shake off filthy images of Aria. There is too much to do for me to be sitting here spanking it, so I finally stand and adjust myself. Walking over to my safe and entering the code, it opens. There are many treasures and tons of money, but I pull out the most valuable piece inside, sliding it into my pocket.

Looking at my watch, I have too much time on my hands so I could use a gym session before I shower.

As I step out of my office to head to my personal gym room in the basement, Nero approaches. "Are you ready, cousin?" He's grinning from ear to ear, knowing that I'm more than anxious for my queen to finally be by my side.

"Born ready."

"Good. I'll be heading home to change. The security is full-on tonight."

"That's great. I refuse to let this evening be ruined. Aria needs to feel welcome and safe in her new home. Now, if you'll excuse me, I need to work off some of this tension."

"Damn—save some load for your wife," he teases, slapping my arm.

"Fuck off. I'm going to the gym. Go get changed. I can't have her see the shitty genetics in parts of my family."

"Hey, I clean up well." He puffs up his chest. We could actually pass for brothers; that's why I'm picking her up, so she doesn't mistake me for Nero or my brother Nico.

I'd hate to have to kill my family if she wanted one of them instead of me. I wouldn't tell them that, though. Needing to cool off, I change and jump into my Olympic-sized swimming pool instead of the weight room. After doing twenty-five laps to feel that burn in every muscle without exhausting myself, I hit the shower.

My dick refuses to simmer down as I lather my body. Giving it some meaningless strokes, I get pissed and turn the temp to icy cold until it goes down. Stepping out with a towel around my waist, I shave my face until it's smooth.

Finally, I slip on my black suit and a red tie to match my queen.

I check myself in my reflection several times because the thought of seeing her is making me anxious. I'm the head of a mafia family, and Aria can bring me to my knees.

I pull out my cell and call Luigi. "We're leaving now."

Finally, I make my way down to my vehicle, sliding in the back while my driver closes the door behind me. With privacy, I turn the cameras on using my phone and hear my queen snapping at her sister. "I'm not getting married to him. I don't care what anyone says." She huffs about the room in a beautiful robe, looking extremely put out.

The entire drive there, I feel the ring in my pocket. Twirling it about in my hand, I know that I'm going to have to slide this fucker on her right now so she understands there's nothing that's going to separate us. It doesn't matter to me how long it takes, but I'll show her that she's mine.

They let me through the gate without hesitation which is wise for the way I'm feeling. "Stay in the vehicle. I'll be back soon," I inform Luigi.

As I arrive and climb the few steps of their portico, Don Grasso comes out.

"Ah, couldn't wait, could you?" Don Grasso chuckles, welcoming me into the house with a wave of his hand toward the entryway.

"I thought I'd give her a proper escort. Besides, I have something to give her." My mind immediately goes to reddening her ass, but I cool my ardor and step inside.

"Well, it's good you came. She's being a little stubborn at the moment." I know all about it, but he doesn't need to be made aware of it.

We shake hands. "As expected, I suppose," I add, knowing Aria wasn't just going to give in so easily. My bride-to-be has an internal flame that I crave. It's in her eyes and I noticed it the first moment our gazes connected. In the two years she's only grown tougher, more determined, and ever more beautiful.

We quietly go up the stairs, and her father knocks on the door while I stand off to the side, so they don't see my feet under the door. Aria's refusal only makes me laugh because my queen has a backbone that I will cherish. However, I'm just going to have to show her mine is made of steel.

2

Aria

"YOU'RE SUCH A BRAT, ARIA," my sister, Gloria, says, crossing her arms and stomping her foot like she's a child instead of a married twenty-two-year-old woman with kids. I'm hardly a brat, but that's hard for anyone to see these days, since they all believe that my fiancé is everything wonderful and powerful.

I flip her off and continue taking my time. "Says the woman who married for love. You got lucky. I get to marry some guy I don't know who is one of the most dangerous men in the world, and probably a big whore to boot." And I'm terrifyingly attracted to Domani Bianchi which only makes matters worse for me. What if I'm putty in his hands? What if I lose who I am?

I'm marrying a man who's so gorgeous it needs to be listed with his other sins. The bastard has the look of a killer meets Superman. Technically we've never met in person, but we've had two close encounters—and one lives so vividly in my head.

Given our family connections and the business they're in, I should have met him more often than that, but I've been locked away since I grew tits and one of my classmates noticed. It happened shortly after my favorite almost meeting with Domani Bianchi. Trying to make a move on me, a classmate, Franco found out the hard way that you don't fuck with a mafia princess. He only got his broken arm as a warning to stay far away. He's lucky it was only that, because my family can be crazy, deadly crazy. He's even luckier that I don't have an older brother. Those motherfuckers in our world are bananas when it comes to their little sisters.

Still, the Bianchis are much worse than that. They run this city and don't hesitate to kill anyone who crosses them. There are other families in the Chicago area, but there's no mistaking who's the true boss. Even my father defers to him. I've heard tail ends of calls that prove how dangerous my future husband can be.

Domani Bianchi's the head of the family now that his father has retired, and now that the dark prince has become king, he's looking for his queen.

From what my mother told me, my dad presented photos to Domani with the mention of my innocence, and the family decided on our marriage. I'm to be his queen in two days here in our family home in front of two hundred strangers from other mafia families. There are four families, but there has been a truce so they will all attend. I've asked to be let out of the marriage, but to no avail. I don't want to be stuck in a loveless marriage. I've already barely seen much of the outside world, and I'm going to miss out, marrying the most ruthless son of a bitch around. Although I wasn't exactly locked away, I became homeschooled and hardly ever spent time with friends over the past two years, so much so that most don't even bother to text me anymore. I've become an outcast when I was the most popular girl. It wasn't the popularity, but rather the loss of having something to look forward to.

Tonight, I'm to meet my husband-to-be at a dinner hosted at his home, where I'll be given a tour of my future residence and all the glorious elegance inside. I rolled my eyes at the way my mother described their home. Shouldn't I have seen it first?

I stare around my insanely massive bedroom, knowing we have an amazing mansion as well. If that's their selling point, it's not a good one. Been there done that kind of thing. Although my room has seen better days. Most of my room has been packed up with boxes lining the walls, signaling my fate is nearly here. I do my best to stay headstrong and resist, but I know my efforts are futile.

My hands are shaking as I brush my hair, avoiding my sister's glare through my large vanity mirror. "Don't you have a family that needs tending to?"

"Don't be a jerk. You're my sister and my family as well. Besides, my husband is getting them ready for bed." I look at my watch. It's a little early for bed, but they have a whole routine that they do no matter where they travel and because her husband is from Ireland, they travel a great deal.

Still, my nerves are on edge, and I wish she'd leave me alone. There's so much that this man could do to me; not only can he physically hurt me if he wants to, but emotionally too. I'm afraid of the butterflies I get in my stomach when I see pictures of him. He's a thousand times more potent when he's near, and in the two years since our last encounter, I can still feel his eyes on me. It's painful the way my body wants to gravitate toward him that elevates my shitty mood. I'm going to be the lovesick puppy while he has whores at his beck and call whenever he deems me not enough.

"Just give him a chance. He's handsome, wealthy, and powerful. Isn't that enough for now? You two haven't even met. What if you both fall in love?"

Scoffing, I stand up and walk over to my bed where she's sitting and plop down beside her, giving her a downward stare. "I highly doubt that. The man will probably make me sick with his affairs."

There's a knock at my bedroom door. "Girls, it's time to go," my papa says.

"We need a few more minutes, Papa," Gloria shouts.

"So unladylike," I whisper with a smirk. She nudges me and sticks out her tongue, proving my point again.

We both hold back a laugh as my father adds, "Domani won't like to be kept waiting." I roll my eyes because I don't give a shit if he doesn't like something. My father's so anxious to hand over the reins of the Grasso family to Domani that he's trying to appease the handsome thug.

"Pity. He'll have to get used to it," I hiss under my breath.

Gloria signs the cross over her chest, kissing the cross she wears. "Heaven help him. He's got his hands full with you."

"Damn right." A deep growl comes from my bedroom door that flies open. I gasp and stare. Domani Bianchi is standing there in my doorway in an all-black suit with a deep blood-red tie, as if he knew I'd be wearing the same red tonight.

"Please leave us," Domani Bianchi orders my sister. His tone is firm, yet not cruel. She doesn't miss a beat and scurries out of the room. "Careful, you're with child, Signora Delaney." She slows down and walks out, closing the door behind her with a smirk on her face, sticking her tongue out at me one more time for good measure.

"Aria." I jerk my eyes away from my bedroom door to his face. The sound of my name off his lips is smooth and rushes over my skin, making my every nerve tingle.

"Yes, that's my name," I inform him with an air of indifference even though my heart's thumping against my breastbone.

He arches his right brow, rakes his gaze over me from head to toe, and then remarks with an upturned lip, "It looks like you have no intention of *coming* tonight." Immediately, I understand he's not talking about his house, but rather, my body. My already heated flesh reddens with lust, and I need more of his sultry voice.

"Oh, I plan to come," I hiss, leaving the sexual innuendo in the air like blood in the water for a dangerous predator. He crosses the distance, leaning over me as I sit on the edge of my bed, and shakes his head. "Just not with you."

"Aria, you won't be coming at all if you keep this up," Domani warns me, inching alarmingly close that I can feel the heat of his body across my skin.

Needing to defuse my body's natural reaction to his magnetism, I clap my hands together excitedly and give him my thousand-watt smile. "Ooh. Does that mean we're not getting married?"

He slides his strong hand down my cheek, feathering his fingers over my throat, and continues to move them down my body. "Oh, we're getting married." Domani's touch is gentle as he loosens the tie on my robe, revealing my bra and panties to his gaze. His eyes return to me, and there's nothing but lust and determination in them. Can he tell that between my clenched thighs the material is drenched?

Gripping my thighs, he nudges them open and then

cups my pussy. His other hand thrusts into my hair, tugging my head back as he leans over me, staring into my eyes. "It's not wise to tease a man on edge, cara mia." His mouth brushes against mine. "Are you going to be a good girl and get dressed?"

"What's in it for me?" I try to hold on to the fight, but his fingers flex, massaging me through my panties.

"Depending on how good of a girl you are, I'll either be making you come with my fingers or my tongue... Or, you can be bad and keep me waiting, but the consequences will be unbearable. You'll be tied up so you can't even touch yourself to get off, Tesoro."

"Ruthless," I moan, flexing my hips forward as I glare at him.

A sinister smile stretches across his handsome face, causing an uptick in my heart rate. "That's right, Aria. Now, go put on that red dress." He points to the black garment bag hanging on the closet door.

"How did you know?"

"Our mothers mentioned it to each other." He presses his lips to my forehead before releasing his grip on my mound. "Remember what I said, Aria. I'm a man of my word." He walks out of the bedroom without stealing another look my way. My panties need to be changed. Asshole. I almost came from that brief encounter. I debate my choices. He doesn't know that I slip my hand under my nightgown to thoughts of him or tease myself in the shower.

Maybe it would be nice to have the king on his knees.

Sexually frustrated, I climb off my bed and begin digging out a new pair of panties. The thing is, half my room has already been packed. I have two days until that sexy beast becomes my husband, and I'm a mess about it. Going into my bathroom, I change and check my hair. It's long with a perfect wave to it. I apply my killer red lipstick—my favorite—and just enough eyeliner and mascara to accentuate my eyes. When I step outside the room, my usual guard is gone and a woman is in his place. "Mrs. Bianchi, I'm your new guard, Torres."

"What happened to John?"

"The boss has changed your guards. I don't know why." We go down the stairs, and Domani is standing there waiting with my parents and my sister. Gloria's husband pops up a minute later. He's the head of the Irish mafia, and it brought a truce to the families when they got together two years ago.

"A start in the right direction," Domani says; he takes my hand, and I feel the metal slide across my finger. It's heavy but warm, as if he's been holding it in his hand this whole time. "Come, now. Let's go. We have a large feast prepared for this special occasion." I do my best not to stare at the diamond that I had on my Pinterest page. It was the only page I was allowed to have, and I went full out on it. It seems so did Domani.

Domani takes my hand, twining our fingers together as my father and mother head out. We're the last to go, and that's when he leans in and whispers, "I'm hoping you're gonna be a really good girl. I want your taste on my tongue." His teeth nip at my earlobe, and shivers run down my body.

He straightens up and mutters to himself, "Fuck, this is going to be a long weekend."

3
_____

Domani

SHE ATTEMPTS to hide her excitement as she looks down at the killer million-dollar ring on her finger. Her eyes meet mine, and I know that she's pleased and surprised. It stiffens my cock to the point of needing readjustment. When her mother addresses her, I take a moment to turn and fix myself. When I face her again, I take her hand in mine and lead her out of the house.

It feels so good to touch her. It's a simple thing that holds so much emotion for me. I bury men for crossing me, but this woman here makes me a marshmallow. She has no idea she has me by the balls. My bride doesn't want to marry me, but I don't give two fucks because one day I'll make her fall in love with me.

Two long years of fighting the urge to claim her as mine. Yes, she was too young for me, but when I saw her, I had no idea that she wasn't an adult. When I learned, I made her father a promise that I'd keep my distance as long as she was to be my queen. Deals made, men warned, and now time is up.

In two days, she'll be my wife, even though she's been my wife in my heart from day one.

It started here on the Grasso estate. Two years later, and I finally get to touch her, taste her, and soon make her mine in every way.

I might have kept her from us actually meeting until today, but I didn't keep my distance, always watching my queen with my men nearby at all times. Twice she nearly fell prey to other men, and I made quick work of them. Aria believes that her father's men broke that kid's arm for daring to touch my queen, but I enjoyed the pleasure myself. His men brought the little fuck to me. If he had kissed her, I'd kill him. Her first kiss belongs to me, so I let him go with a warning to stay away from her or I'd make his subsequent punishment permanent.

I assist her into the vehicle before taking the seat beside her as my driver closes the door behind me. My eyes linger on Aria as she adjusts her dress that rode up as she sat down on the leather. "You look stunning, Aria."

She whips her head my way and smiles. "Thank you, Mr. Bianchi."

"It's Domani, amore mia." A scowl comes over her face before she softens it and sits closer to me. That's good, because it's what I want.

"Domani," she purrs intentionally against my ear. "Just so you know...I'm not gonna play nice with the devil. If you betray me with another woman, I'll gladly cut off your dick and serve it to her for dinner." The deadly warning off her lips is an aphrodisiac. Fuck, I love this woman more and more with every passing day.

Cupping her head and turning it so we're face to face, I

lean in less than an inch from her red lips and answer her, "I know, cara mia. That's why you're the one I want for my queen." I let go before I take this to a place that will have her impaled on my cock.

She doesn't sit back but stares at me with her brow arched. "Just letting you know that's the only warning you'll get. Now, do they plan to drive, or are they waiting for us to start fucking in the back seat," she finishes with a huff, sitting properly in her seat with her back firmly against the leather with her arms folded under her breasts.

"You have a mouth on you." One I plan to do a lot with. There have been many nights, days, and showers where I've pictured her on her knees servicing me, begging me to fuck that pretty mouth.

She tilts her head slightly with a saccharinely sweet smirk. "I'm glad you noticed."

I want to wipe that attitude off her face. "I've noticed so much more, Aria. I promise I've noticed every single thing." Licking my lips, I rake my eyes over her entire body. She becomes flustered, so I tap on the divider and my driver pulls out of their driveway. The rest of the family follows behind with their own security. I wanted time alone with her, but it's a fucking mistake. My cock weeps with the urge to be deep inside her, and now she fucking knows what she's doing to me.

Stealing glances at her, I watch as she shifts uncomfortably in her seat, playing with the hem of her dress, which draws my eyes to the spot right between her legs.

"So, is your whole family going to be there?" She breaks the heated silence, causing my head to jolt up to look at her face.

"My parents, brother, and cousin will be there with the guards, but not the entire Bianchi family."

"Isn't that dangerous?"

"Our estate is well secured. I wouldn't risk your safety like that." I take her hands and bring them to my lips for a kiss.

"Okay." She's nervous, but I'm not sure it's all because of me.

"I want you to relax, Aria." I sweep her hair behind her ear, seeing the diamond earrings that she got for her eighteenth birthday—a gift from my mother to her future daughter-in-law.

"Sorry, I haven't been outside in a long time."

"I know. I'm sorry. I'll make it up to you." I brush my hand down her soft cheek. Her gorgeous caramel eyes look at me with a bit of hope. She doesn't understand the depths of my obsession, and it's wise that she doesn't know until we're married. Maybe a long time after that. My fidelity is guaranteed.

"How far is your estate?" She plays with her ring, trying to look at it without looking shocked. I hope she loves it; then again, I knew she would.

"Twenty minutes. And it's your estate as well," I remind her. Everything I have is hers.

"We're not married yet." The attitude is back in a heartbeat, as if talking about the wedding sets her teeth on edge.

I love her too much to think straight sometimes. I try to hold back the anger, but I snip out, "It's a forgone conclusion, Aria. Get used to it."

She looks out the window, avoiding my gaze, and I see that she's upset. Fuck, I can't let her cry.

"You'll like it there. I promise."

"Who lives there?"

"Just my parents and me. We have our own wing."

"So you still live with your parents?" she teases, knowing it's customary for many families to be close.

"Yes. I do. I haven't moved out of the family home. I'm such a disgrace, but at least they haven't relegated me to the basement," I answer playfully.

"It's a shame. I don't know if this is going to work between us." I don't know if she's playing anymore, and I don't care. Any mention of us not being together is unacceptable.

I growl and flip her onto my lap with her legs straddling my thighs, her breasts firmly against my chest and her face inches from mine. "Aria Grasso, in two days, you'll be my wife. Enough talk about it not happening, because it is. Do you understand me? I don't like to repeat myself." I tug on her hair at the base of her skull, tilting her head. Dragging my tongue along the column of her throat, I suck lightly on her pulse, feeling it thumping against my lips.

"So tell me, Aria. What is happening in two days?"

"We're getting married."

"Good answer." I drag her head down to mine and kiss her parted lips, slipping my tongue inside possessively, dominating her mouth. Pulling her away gently, I growl, "Perfect answer." The car hits a pothole and our bodies grind hard, adding to the growing need to be inside of her.

"Sorry, sir."

"It's okay," I grunt.

"Yes, it is," she moans, rolling her hips on my length and looking like a goddess as she does.

"Fuck, I'm doing my best not to take you. Be a good girl."

"I thought you said if I was a good girl, you'd make me come."

"Okay. You've been a good girl so far. One for now." I grip her hips and rock her pussy onto my bulge, allowing her dress to ride up and reveal a pair of white panties—not the pretty pink ones she had on earlier. "You changed your panties."

"You got them all dirty."

"I'm about to dirty these ones as well." I free my cock from my slacks and pull her panties to the side, slipping my cock between the material, skimming along her lips. "Ride my length. Work your orgasm out, my queen." We move faster and faster until she cries out my name. I snatch her lips in a deep kiss as I shoot my load all over her mound.

"Aria, amore mia."

"We're pulling up to the gate, sir." The car slows down. I lift her off me, fixing her panties and pulling her dress down back in place.

"Thank you, Luigi." It takes a minute to get from the gate to the front of the house, so I have time to tuck myself away, sticky and wet, smiling like a king. I steal a glance at my bride, who's flushed and running her hands through her hair to look a little more presentable. I take one hand and kiss it. "And thank you, Aria."

"Thank you. I guess being a good girl has its benefits."

"I'm glad you see it my way." I kiss her lips once more before the vehicle comes to a complete stop, and she reaches for the door, but I stop her. "Wait." I get out first and take her hand. As she steps out, I drag her to my side. "Come, Aria."

"I did," she whispers as her body slams into mine. She pushes away just enough to look like a respectable couple.

"Don Grasso, Signora Grasso, welcome to our home."

"Thank you, Dom."

We head into the house to be greeted by my eager

parents. They've kept their distance from my bride as well. "It's a pleasure to finally meet you, Aria. You are lovely."

"Thank you." There are a bunch of questions going through Aria's head because, as far she knows, the plans for our marriage have only been in the works for two weeks. My mother has been planning for the past six months with Aria's mother. My sweet wife has only been legal for two weeks.

"Mama, please let her breathe. Remember, in two days, she'll be here with us every day." Aria stiffens a bit, and I pull her tighter to my side, massaging her arm in slow circles.

"Sorry. I'm excited." I love my mother, and I can't blame her for the excitement. I'm ready to have her here forever.

"Ignacia, come—let me show you my latest designs," my mother says to hers. They have been acquainted for a long time.

"Girls, do you want to come with us?" Mrs. Grasso asks Aria and her sister, Gloria. I hold back my need to cling to Aria and release my hold when Gloria grabs her hand.

"Sure. Let's give the guys time to bullshit," Gloria says, winking at her husband.

4

Domani

"Who needs a drink?" my father asks as soon as all the ladies leave the room.

"I sure as hell can use one," Don Grasso says. We walk to the living room where my father has a wet bar. Just as we circle it, the Don leans in and adds, "Just so you know—if you do anything to hurt her, our families will go to war."

"I'll never give her a reason to be upset," I admit. I'm too damned in love to see her hurting.

"Please. We're men with prices put on our heads by our competitors. She will be upset every time you leave," Cormack Delaney adds in his thick Irish accent. Gloria and Cormack met in Ireland and have been attached ever since.

"Well, I will do my best to make her happy and take out all my enemies before they can get me."

"What can I get you, gentlemen?" my father asks to break up the conversation. Every one of us knows the dark side of our lives and that risk comes with rewards.

"Do you have Maker's?" Don Grasso asks.

"Sure do." Steps behind the bar, pulling out the glasses and setting them on the bar top. My father is proud of his collection, making sure to have plenty of the common ones for his guests.

"I'll have the same, Pops."

"Same for me," Delaney calls out, checking his phone again. This is the second time I saw him on it in a matter of minutes.

"Everything okay?" I ask Delaney.

He lifts his head and with a smile, says, "Yes, just checking the monitor on the little ones." He shows me the screen of his little boys sleeping.

"Damn. Paranoid," I remark, knowing damned well that I'll be worse.

He laughs, taking a drink before saying, "I never had a soft spot until I met Gloria. Now, I'll do anything to protect them."

Grasso clasps his hand on Delaney's shoulder, smiling at his son-in-law. "Good. My grandbabies are well protected, but I worry as well."

"I'm still worried about my boys, and they're grown men," my father adds. I know it's true because he's been on me about my obsession.

"Where is your other son?" Don Grasso asks.

"He'll be coming soon. The boy lives with his head in the books." Niccolò's one hell of an accountant. He works to keep us out of prison, making sure nothing ties us to illegal activity.

"That's really good. I wish I had sons, but the girls are my angels."

"Maybe we'll get lucky with tons of bambinos."

"This one is already working on it," he mutters, nudging Delaney while glaring at me.

"Lucky fucker," I say under my breath.

"Damn right. Soon, I'm sure you two will fill this mansion with a horde of little ones."

"Two more days." I down my glass, barely swallowing before adding, "Do you think we should check on them?"

"No. They're fine, just like you told your mother. Relax. In two days, she'll be here forever." My father-in-law laughs before taking a drink of his whiskey. Everyone finds my misery hilarious, but if he keeps fucking with me, I'll have Aria locked up in our bedroom for months too busy taking my dick to visit her parents, and I'll let him know it too.

My phone buzzes in my inside jacket pocket. "Excuse me." I step away from them and pull it out, and it's Nero, my second-in-command and cousin.

"Get everyone to safety. Someone's lurking outside. I'm going to check it out." Shots fire in the distance as he hangs up.

"Get Aria into the safe room," I bark out to Luigi who's standing guard at the entryway. He immediately takes off and runs to their location.

"What the hell is going on?"

"Yeah. Bianchi what's happening?"

It's a surprise to find someone lurking outside the exterior on the cameras. I get up and call the front security at the gate. It rings and rings. I pull up the surveillance cameras on my phone and see that several of my guys are running out of the gates. "Someone's shooting at my men." I glare at the two other men in the room who aren't blood, feeling suddenly suspicious of them.

I pull out my gun and run straight down to the fucking front. My security gate team has been shot. One's dead, and the other is bleeding out. I call the ambulance as Delaney and the Don come following. We secure the area with my other ten men that circle the perimeter. The intruder can't get inside, but they shot through the gate.

I'm hot—ready to bust some heads and throw salt in the wounds.

"Shit, where is Niccolò?"

My father pulls out his cell and calls him. He's talking to him, so thank fuck for that.

"I haven't had a problem in years. Now that I bring my bride here, someone attacks?"

"I believe someone doesn't want our families to be tied together." Grasso is right, but none of the families have even hinted at the alignment between the Grasso and Bianchi Families.

"Who? This has been in motion for years," I remind him.

"I don't know, but until we do, it's best to be on high alert."

"Where's Nico?" I ask. He's supposed to be here any fucking minute. If that fucker finds him before he's somewhere safe...I just can't even think of that.

"He was just leaving his condo. He'd gotten carried away with work."

A sense of relief fills me, but everything isn't said and done for the night. "Sounds like him. Did you tell him to stay there as well?"

"Hell, yeah. The boy doesn't need to get into this." My father checks his gun as we stalk together to check on our women. I have to hold Aria and promise I'll make it better.

"Fucking hell. Who would be that stupid?" I look at the footage as we head to the safe room, but all I can think about is getting to Aria. Maybe that's my motherfucking problem; I've been too fucking stuck in the clouds to see the enemy creeping in.

I punch in the code, and the door slides open. Everyone

enters before I do, but we find all our women comforting each other. Their eyes turn to us and they run to their men, and then it's just Aria, who gasps.

"You're okay," Aria cries out, throwing her arms around me. Fuck, I feel like a king just to have an ounce of her concern.

I kiss her temple and hair before I answer her. "Yes, amore. I'm well, but two of my men have been injured." I leave out that one is dead because I don't want to upset her any more than necessary. "You're staying here tonight where I know you'll be secure until we have this under control."

"I need to get to my boys, but I want Gloria here until I come back with them," Cormack says, staring at me with the warning that he's trusting me with her safety. I nod, answering his unspoken request.

"All of you will stay here tonight. This isn't random," I answer.

"Do you know who it is?" Aria looks up at me with a fear that pisses me off.

Cupping her face, I stare into her gorgeous eyes. "No, but I will. Nothing and no one will stop our wedding," I tell her, but it's for everyone just in case they get any crazy ideas of canceling it.

My phone rings, and it's Nero. "What do you have?"

"He's gone. It's definitely a guy with brass balls. We're waiting for a medic and the fucking fire department out in the woods." He's breathing heavily as he spits it out for me.

"What the hell happened?"

"We gave chase, and the asshole had a trip wire set up with rigged explosives. We've lost two more guys." I could put a bullet in this bastard's head, but we need to make him earn his death.

"When we find this asshole, his death will be slow and painful. Do what you need to do. Are you good, though?"

"Yeah, I'm a little slower than these guys," he huffs. That's when I realize he's still catching his breath.

He's fast, but not sprinter fast. "That's because you're built like a tank. Stay safe."

"I told you," Aria huffs, slapping my chest as tears stream down her gorgeous face.

"You did. Did you know something, Aria?" It's a stupid question, but maybe she heard something without understanding what it meant.

"Of course not. I don't leave my ivory tower, but we've all gotten together and someone who hates us knew it. It doesn't take much intelligence," she sasses, rolling her eyes at me.

"Handful," Gloria mutters.

"She's still worth it." I place a soft kiss on her lips. "Stay in the house. I have to get to the bottom of this."

"Please don't get yourself killed," Aria pleads, filling me with unexplainable vigor and determination. Nothing's going to stop me from getting back to her.

"Not gonna happen. I have a bride waiting for me."

My phone rings and it's Luigi, on top of being my personal guard and driver, he's one of my security experts. "We've got a hit on the vehicle he fled in, but it's been reported stolen this morning."

That's not what I like to hear, but given the situation, it's to be expected. "Shit. Okay. Well, get any city cameras of this fucker. I want this bastard taken care of before the wedding."

"Already on it. Our connection in the city is scanning all the systems for it."

"Call me when he has something."

"Yes, boss."

"Hey—next time, don't go running into danger like that, Dom," Don Grasso says. "You could have been shot if he'd gotten over the walls."

"The sensors would have gone off. Fuck. I hate that fucking front gate. It's a hazard, leaving us at risk." It's for aesthetics, but it's useless when it comes to protection. In all my years this house has never come under attack because the families would be too fucking stupid.

"We could have been shot at before we arrived. This was intentional."

"All of the vehicles are bulletproof," I explain to Aria, but does the shooter know that? Probably. It's only wise for us to own several armor-plated rides.

I look over her head and to her father whose tension is visibly high. "We need to go back to your home. I wonder if someone has been lurking around your house at a distance and followed us here. We weren't home for more than thirty minutes before all hell broke out."

"Do you believe this has to do with us?" he questions, teeth clenching, knuckles whitening. The old man better chill out or he's going to have a heart attack.

"It might have to do with Aria. Her guard was missing this morning. Have you located him? I haven't been able to get a hold of him. That's why I added one of my mother's guards to guard Aria's room."

"I was made aware of that, but he hadn't called in sick. I thought you pulled him for your own reasons." He's referring to my jealousy when it comes to his daughter—my bride.

"No. I trusted him to keep his eyes to himself." He's been protecting her for years and has never given me a reason to

believe he wanted her. Still, if this is his handiwork, I'll kill
that fucker without a second thought.

"Maybe," her father scoffs.

My phone goes off as we get into my SUV. It's her room
sensor. I see the little fuck in there and his face is familiar,
but it's not John or even Cormack, who should almost be at
the house. I don't share that with her father because then
he'll know I had cameras in her room and that I've seen
much more of his daughter than I should have. Technically,
the legal age in this state is seventeen. Still, I don't think he'd
appreciate it. I said my obsession with her is sick. I'm a
fucking mobster; it's not like I live on the right side of the
law anyway.

"The cameras are going off. Someone's on my property,"
her father says as we head down the road.

"Maybe it's Delaney?"

"No. He has the passcode to go through the gate." He
makes a call as I drive like a madman. "Delaney, be careful.
My silent sensors just went off. Okay." They talk for a
minute.

"What happened?"

"He's almost there, and the boys are in the safe room
there with their nanny." I can see the panic in his eyes.
They're his little grandbabies, and it's turning that fear into
an animalistic rage. Grasso has been one hell of a Don, but
with age and a happy family, he's slowed his businesses.

"Good."

My phone rings again as we get closer to the house. I put
it on speaker. "What have you got, Luigi?"

"We've got him ID'd. It's Franco Tortelli, the kid that
tried to kiss her and you broke his arm." He didn't need to
finish that last bit. I'd never forgotten his name. Anyone that
dares to defile my queen is on my hit list. I should have

finished him off back then, but he was just some punk kid who had a crush.

"What? Are you fucking serious?"

"Shit. He's gone off the deep end. We're on this way to his apartment, and we're going to wait to see if he shows up."

"Good. Bring him to me if he does."

"I'm going to take my time with him," Grasso says, clenching his fists. We arrive at their gated residence and see Delaney. Rage is apparent as hell on his face as he holds both of his boys in his arms. Three of his men are surrounding him and the boys.

Through gritted teeth, he snarls, "He's inside. My men have him tied down. Have your way."

We enter the house and go straight to the sound of someone struggling. When we do, I see the little bitch on the ground, tied up and still struggling. I swiftly kick him in the balls, watching him crumble and squeal like a little bitch.

I grab his collar and drag him onto a chair. "You fucked up, Franco, buddy. You had the nerve to come to my home, kill my men, and scare my bride. You're either nuts, or fucking stupid. Either way, you've sealed your fate."

He spits at me through his busted lip. "She deserves someone better than you."

I shrug and chuckle lightly. "She does, but that's not your business."

Grasso interrupts, itching with violence in his eyes. "It's mine, and I've given this man my blessing. Who are you to deem otherwise?"

"She loved me, and we were supposed to be together."

Wow. I laugh harder because he's got a few screws loose. "This guy's nuts. She didn't love you, and I know that."

"He's fucking pathetic and a bit crazy. My daughter

wouldn't give you the time of day. She was freaked out and felt grossed out that you nearly put your mouth on her."

"I should have killed you then," I remind him that I'd granted him mercy.

"Maybe, but if I can't have her, neither can you." He swings his legs, trying to stab me with a hidden knife in his shoe, but he's not quick enough and I break his ankle, causing him to scream like music to my ears.

"Nice try," I add, dropping his leg.

A gun goes off, and I snap my head toward my father-in-law, who's smirking. "Sorry. I was getting tired of the little prick."

That's when I notice his shirt. It reads *Tick Tock, Motherfucker*. I don't know what it means, but it sends a chill up my spine. "No need to apologize. I'm ready to get back to my woman. Let's get some things and head back."

"They're gonna freak when they see the blood on us. Let's go wash up."

"Good idea." We barely make it into the hallway toward the stairs when the house goes off in an explosion, sending us falling backward, and the world goes black.

5

Aria

"Where are they?" I sigh, freaking out more and more as time ticks by, wringing my fingers as I sit down and get up again to pace the room. It's been two hours since they left the estate. They should have been back. I stare at Cormack, who looks calm.

"What the hell happened, honey?" Gloria asks her husband. I stop and wait for him to explain where my father and fiancé are.

He shrugs like it's not a big deal when I'm ready to jump out of my skin. "I don't know. They were going inside the house to get the guy that my team had bagged and gagged believing he's the guy who was here. Maybe they went to work on him." So what he's saying is they probably took him somewhere to torture and kill him.

"Well, why don't you call them and find out?" I snap, getting in his face. Gloria gently takes my hand and leads me to a chair.

I stare at my brother-in-law as he dials. It feels like

forever as he goes through contact after contact, but Cormack doesn't get an answer until he tries the last guy. It's muffled and loud as he puts it on speakerphone because he can't hear him.

"Boss, explosion," a voice groans out. Did he say explosion? I swear the room tilts a bit, but I press my hand on the armrest.

"No talking. Get this man to the hospital. Who is this?" a male voice snarls on the phone.

"Who the hell is this?" Cormack barks out.

"This is Chief Miller from the CFD." The fire department is at our house?

"What happened to Danny?"

"We had an explosion. Several men dead." Oh my God. I did hear him correctly.

"No," I cry out, standing because I need air.

Stumbling toward the front door, the following words cause me to freeze. "Are there any survivors?" Cormack asks.

"Not that we can tell." The world goes black and I crumble, falling into someone's arms as I lose consciousness.

"Wake up, amore mia." I swear I hear Domani, but it must be a dream. The feel of his strong hand sliding over my cheek wakes me up. I press my face into his hold to remember his touch in my soul.

"Domani, you're alive," I call out as my eyes focus on his face. Tears flow freely down my face.

"Yes—no one can take me away from you. I told you that. Please, amore, don't cry." I do my best to rein in the tears, but it's the opposite. He holds me to his chest, breathing in my scent as he steals kisses on the crown of my head.

Finally gaining control of my emotions, I pull back slightly to look up into his rugged mug. "Where am I?"

"In our bedroom," he growls with a smirk.

Lust shoots through my veins, and I let him know it as I hum, "Got me right where you want me, don't you?"

"Yes, but we still have a day before I make you my wife." He releases his hold on me and backs off the bed. I take him in for the first time, and I'm shocked. He's covered in dried blood, his clothes filthy and his face caked with dirt.

"Oh my goodness, you look bad. What are you doing here? You should see a doctor."

"I'm fine," he says, brushing off my concern.

"My dad," I screech, jumping up. I forgot he went with him. Domani grabs my arms, holding me firmly in place.

"Calm down. He's good, showering and then resting. Your mother's tending to him." He lets go of me and then removes his suit jacket. "Dinner's waiting for us, so as soon as I get out of the shower, we'll eat. I could really use some food and need to make sure you're well fed." He strolls to the bathroom like it's nothing, while I have a hundred and twenty questions.

"What happened?" I call out, walking toward the bathroom. My heels are gone but I'm still in my dress, which has shifted a bit. I adjust it and ask again, "What happened, Domani?"

He cups my face and kisses my forehead. "We managed to avoid the biggest part of the blast." He shakes his head. "That guy was fucking nuts."

"Who was he? Why was he after you?"

"It was the guy whose arm I broke for trying to kiss you." I gasp. *Did he?* He blanches from the slip.

"You broke his arm?" I ask, because the incident happened two years ago, shortly before I was pulled from the school.

A knock at the door interrupts his response. "Yes?" he calls toward the door, getting out of my interrogation.

"Domani, I need to see you."

"Okay, Mama." He walks past me and goes to the door.

The second he opens the door, she throws her arms around him and cries. "I almost lost you." Has he not seen her already? "Damn it, you need to be more careful." She slaps his chest, making him groan. "Now get in the shower, eat, and then the doc will see you later."

She walks past him, pulling me down to sit next to her on the edge of the bed. Brushing my hair away from my face, she asks so sweetly, "Are you well, dear? You gave Domani a good scare."

"He gave me one, too," I complain with a slight smile on my face. When I look, he's heading into the shower, closing the door. Slick fucker. Still, my mind has a million questions that I will get answered in good time.

"You two are going to be hilariously cute together."

"Thank you. I should get up and go eat with everyone."

"Actually, everyone has decided to eat in their rooms. After this drama, Gloria and her husband are holding their babies close for the night. Your parents are resting, and I must tend to my husband, so you and Domani actually will just be dining together. "

A knock comes against the door frame. "Dinner, Signoras."

"Come in." The chef brings in a tray with two other servers.

"Please enjoy, Mrs. Bianchi." I realize he's speaking to

me. "This is not how I planned to serve my first dinner to you, but alas, things can't be perfect all the time."

"It smells fabulous."

"Grazie. If you should need anything, please do not hesitate. I am Giuseppe," he says.

"Grazie, Giuseppe."

"I hope you two have a pleasant night. Get some rest. We have a big day tomorrow," his mother says, brushing a kiss to my temple before standing.

"Yes, Mrs. Bianchi."

"Come, Giuseppe. I'm sure they want to eat in private." He leaves with her, and his staff goes with him. She closes the door with a goodnight.

"Goodnight."

That's when I process that the shower has turned off. I don't know how long it's been that way until the door opens, and Domani is just in his towel that's snugly wrapped around his waist. He has another towel that he's running through his thick dark hair. Muscles bulge from his biceps, creating a compelling picture. His broad chest has a spattering of hair across his killer pectorals and down to his taut abs, making a happy trail to his large cock that's jerking under the cloth material. I'm practically panting in heat. My thighs clench shut as I stare.

"Amore, stop looking at me naked. I'm doing my best to wait until our wedding day."

"Dom...sorry. Um...I just didn't expect you to be so... gorgeous," I confess.

With a growl, he adds, "Give me a minute." He steps into his closet out of sight and comes back a minute later in a pair of sweats and a tee-shirt, adding a different element to his sexy. Who knew a man like him owned regular clothes?

"Come on. Let's eat before it gets cold. Giuseppe wouldn't want you to be upset with his cooking."

"Okay." I climb off the bed and walk around to the small table in his room, taking a seat across from him. I've never eaten in front of him before. In fact, everything about this man is new to me, except the years of fantasizing about him.

"Eat, Aria. When we say our vows, you will be too busy for food for a long while. Do get your nourishment in now." I lift up the lid to my plate to hide my blush when it comes to us fucking. When I look at my dish, it's one of my favorites—Pappardelle in a beef and mushroom sauce. Looking up at Domani, I wonder if he knew it was my favorite. "You can learn a lot about someone from their Pinterest posts."

"I can't believe you did this for me."

He pours a glass of wine for both of us. I don't drink a lot of wine, but at a good dinner, my parents let me have a bit. "It's nothing. I don't cook the food; still, I am glad you are pleased. Now, do eat." He begins to dip his bread into the sauce before taking a large bite of the pasta.

"This is delicious. I think I'm in love." I moan, taking another bite.

"Hey, don't get Giuseppe killed, now," he growls, taking a drink of his wine.

"Silly, I meant the dish. I better continue running every day or I'll be getting chunky."

"You can run if you please, but it must be in the gym here. I do not trust your safety."

"I know. I prefer the treadmill anyway. It's not like I've been let out much since that day with Franco."

He pauses with his fork midair. "No talk of him tonight, please. I'd like to enjoy my dinner, cara mia."

"Yes, sorry. So when you're not all mob bossing and stuff, what do you do for fun?"

"Fun? I watch television or read books. What about you?"

I shoot my brow up at him and then shake my head before taking a sip of my drink. "I'm guessing you already know that, but I'll humor you." Setting the glass down, I continue. "I like to draw and paint. Nothing fancy, just stuff to occupy my time outside of my schoolwork, and well, pure boredom."

His face lights up. "Are those your drawings on Pinterest?"

"Yes. I've had offers and requests, but they're just for me."

"Well, they are lovely. I especially love the girl staring out her window with a whimsical look, as if waiting on her lover."

I gasp. "Is that what you see?"

"I do. Is that not what it is?"

I smile widely. "No, you're a hundred percent correct on it. Some think she's depressed, miserable."

"They miss the slightest glint in her eyes or the upturn of her lips."

"Thank you, Domani. I'm glad someone truly enjoyed it."

"I'm sure there are many others that caught it."

"No one I know. You're the first person that actually took a real interest in my art."

"I'd like that piece to be somewhere special in the house. Wherever, even if you just put it in our bedroom."

"Are you serious?"

"Tesoro, I am always serious. I don't say things I don't mean."

"Oh God, the explosion," I sob. "Everything I had was in my art studio in the back of the house."

"Do not worry. Your studio is safe. Your father said he knew they meant the world to you. My men will collect everything tomorrow. That part of the house was clear of the fire, so they haven't been damaged. It was only in the main front living area."

"That's really good. I'd been so worried about you two that I'd completely forgotten about them."

"Thank you, Aria." He squeezes my hand and then continues to eat. I do the same because I am pretty damn hungry and the smell is incredible. By the time we're done stuffing our faces, I sit back and sigh.

"I think I overate. I'm stuffed."

"You needed it. You haven't eaten most of the day."

"How did you know that?"

"I asked earlier." I know he's lying, but I let it go.

"You know you could have just talked to me to learn my likes and dislikes."

"Yes, but you've seen what happens when I have you alone and close to me." He takes my hand and gently massages my wrist with his thumb.

"We have very nice talks," I offer.

"Smart ass." I let out a yawn. "How about we watch some television and then go to bed?"

"Okay." He hops up and grabs the remote from his dresser and turns on the television. He has it on a *CSI* marathon—the original *CSI* with William Peterson, my favorite. "How about this?"

"I do like this one—even if it's a cop show."

"If it makes you feel better, I used to watch *Cops* all the time as a teenager." He shakes his head at me after I press my hand to my chest in shock.

"That's funny. Oh, the irony," I remark dramatically. A criminal loving a criminal-catching show.

"Do you have a good enough view from there?" he asks.

"Yes." I'm totally lying, and he can read it. In a swift motion, he picks me up and sits me on the bed. "That's much better."

He sits on the edge of the bed, but from the looks of things, I have a feeling he's not going to be joining me. Cupping my face, he asks, "Amore, are you going to be okay in here alone? I have to talk to my men. With everything that has happened, I have a mess to clean up."

As much as I hate for him to leave me, I know that just because the threat is gone, it doesn't mean their work is over. "Do what you have to do. I'll be okay here. Just be safe, please, Domani." He bends over and kisses my lips. We start off sweet and gentle, but before I know it, he has pinned me to the pillows and his mouth devours mine. His hands wander all over my body, skimming up my thighs, and then he pulls back. We're both panting, filling our lungs with much-needed air. Straightening himself up, Domani adjusts his cock, which is clearly beyond hard in his joggers. "You have no idea how sexy you are."

"I'm starting to see." I lick my lips, teasing Domani and myself because I'm so damned aroused as well.

"That's a bad girl. Keep that up, and you won't be coming tonight."

"Fine. I need to shower since someone left me a sticky mess, but I'm guessing you didn't grab any of my clothes."

"No. I didn't, but your mom picked out some new clothes for your new life by my side. They're in the closet on the right." My eyes shoot open wide, shock and excitement written all over my face.

Climbing onto my knees, I throw my arms around his

neck for a huge hug that he returns, lifting me off the bed. I kiss his cheek as he sets me back on the mattress. "You are a big surprise, Mr. Bianchi."

"We've only just begun, Aria, but I must go." He kisses me once more before he rushes from the room. As soon as the door shuts, I hop off the bed. I have to pee and shower, so I scurry into his impressive bathroom. I scope out his double sink and see he has my favorite soaps already stocked. He hasn't left anything out. I dig through the cabinets and see female products for me. My mother must have given him a list or maybe she sent out one of her people to run around and get everything. Damn, I wonder why I bothered to pack in the first place.

Turning on the shower, I strip and test the water. It's perfectly warm. The spray is so refreshing after all that's happened today. As I'm washing my hair, I remember that the door's not locked. I don't feel comfortable with it unlocked, so I hurry up and rinse off. Stealing a large fluffy towel off the shelf, I wrap my body up and pull out another for my hair.

We have the same luxury as this at home, but it's different because this will be mine soon, and it's incredible. This home is where I'm supposed to raise a family. It's *surreal*. That's the word that I've been looking for since Domani stepped through my bedroom door, growling and demanding. Two years of peering through my imagination for that one moment in time when our eyes met through a doorway. It was a moment so long ago that I wonder if I'd just made it all up. I remember hearing my father say that he wasn't even supposed to be there.

I slip into the closet, looking for the clothes, and everything I need is inside. My mother wasted no time filling it up with all my favorite things. I see other things that I wouldn't have considered, but since I'm going to be a married woman, these pretty nighties are something I could get used to, especially with a husband who wants to devour me.

I grab one off the hanger and slide it over my head, and then pull a pair of panties out. Although I'm not sure what the point is, since they'll be ruined the second I start thinking about him and his muscular body, passionate lips, and talented mouth.

As much as I'd prefer to go without undies, I'm afraid someone will come in. Shimmying them up my legs, I see my reflection in his floor-length mirror, and I look fucking sexy. Maybe I should change.

"Nah." I climb back into bed and snuggle under the covers.

6

Domani

LEAVING THE BEDROOM AND, more importantly, Aria was a test of wills. If I didn't have an empire to get under control, I would have stayed with my woman. I meet my men on the stairs. "Stay outside the door. Don't go in there for any reason."

"Yes, boss." The door locks on its own, but that doesn't mean she can't open it from the inside and they could come in that way. My men don't enter my bedroom for any reason, but when it comes to Aria, I don't trust many. She's beautiful, enchanting, and my only weak spot. If anyone wants to get at me, she'd be the target. It kills me to even consider something fucked up like that, but it's the life we're living.

Nero meets me at the bottom of the stairs. "How is she?"

"Good, but we have a lot to deal with right now so I can't focus on my queen."

"Very well. Our men have been taken to the funeral home. The company for the gate has been contacted, and

I'm sure we can get them out tomorrow." We walk to my office, closing the door behind us.

Walking over to my liquor cabinet, I pull out a bottle of bourbon. Waving it at him, he nods. I pour us a glass and then take a seat behind my desk. "I want it completely reinforced. What about the fires?"

"The fire department got it under control, but the damage was significant."

"Have a crew come to level it out. We'll add a helipad there instead. I thought it protected us, but it backfired."

"Yes. We're relocating any animals found alive?"

"Yes, of course. Either to the local zoos or to another forest preserve. I'm ruthless, but ecosystems matter."

"Good. I'm going to see if we have room for any in the garden. My mother and Aria like animals."

"You have your own Snow White." He nudges me with his elbow.

"That I do. Have the families been contacted?" I question, returning to business. I want to get back to Aria as soon as humanly possible.

"We were waiting on you before we made the calls."

Nodding, I add, "That's good. It's best that it comes from me."

"That's what we figured."

"Give me all the numbers and contacts for each man." He pulls out a piece of paper from his suit jacket.

"Niccolò sent it over about ten minutes ago. He wants you to call him when you get a chance. He's pissed he wasn't here to fight."

"He's always itching to prove himself more than just my accountant. He's even working out now more and more." I shake my head and down my glass. Nero stands and brings the bottle over to my desk. "Grazie."

I pour myself another glass, drinking about half and topping it off again. "Take it easy. You've got a lot of calls to make."

"That's what I'm gonna need this for. Crying mothers I'm not prepared for."

"I bet. You know...maybe Niccolò's found a girl."

"I wonder. I should ask him if there's someone he's interested in."

"It would be nice. Then he might not be so damned uptight." That's my little brother for sure. Great at numbers, terrible with people. We love him, and he's a tough bastard, but heaven help him if he has to speak to anyone. The man just hates talking at all costs.

"Well, I'm going to steal a piece of apple pie. It's fresh out of the oven. Do you want one?" Nero has a huge sweet tooth, especially when it comes to baked goods.

"Sure, but be careful Giuseppe doesn't see you, or you'll lose a finger."

"I'll tell him it's for you." We both chuckle as he walks out.

Then I go about making the calls. After I finish the first one, Nero comes in, letting me know the police are outside and want to speak with me. I nod and have them come into my living room. "Yes, Detective Sims, to what do I owe this extremely late visit?"

"I'm stopping by to inform you that my team has already ruled that you acted in self-defense. And that Tortelli was a fucking nut."

"That's for sure. Thank you for that. It's been a long night, so if that's all you have, I have to make some important calls to my guards' families in Italy."

"Oh. Yes. Good luck with that." He stands, and Nero escorts him out. From the footage I gave them, they were able to see that those who died had been attacked by a mad man. The explosion to his body had been so intense that only fragments could be gathered. Thankfully, the bullet to the heart had been untraceable because his heart couldn't be found.

Two attacks on two reputed crime families were shocking and people would believe it was a hit from one of the other families, which will keep them off our tails. It's not as if they want to get entangled in all of this mess. Besides, we have the right people in our pockets to look the other way.

Most of the people killed didn't have family in the States, so I had to make calls to Italy. Not pleasant, but there isn't much I can do. Their people will be compensated as best we can. I'll leave that to my accountant Niccolò to handle.

Making it up to the bedroom, I unlock the door and see my bride-to-be with the covers just below her ass, the perfect view to come home and see. I growl, stripping out of my clothes and climbing into bed in just my boxers.

I slide under the covers and pull Aria to me. "Domani," she sighs. That's what I want to hear.

"Sleep, my queen," I command. She smiles, and I feel her body relax. "I love you, Aria." I know she can't hear me, but I have to say it.

"My king," she utters.

"That's right. Now and forever."

I wake up four hours later to the feel of Aria grinding on my cock with her round ass. Growling her name along the shell of her ear, I grip her hips and stop her. She startles, waking up. "Aria, you're a bad little girl."

"Sorry, I don't know what came over me." There's a blush on her cheeks like she's embarrassed, but I know she's flushed from desire because her wicked eyes are full of mischief. God, I want to possess this woman so painfully.

"I'm about to come all over you if you keep it up," I grit out, aching to fuck her this instant.

"You make it sound like a bad thing."

"We're not married yet," I insist. I won't give in now that I'm so fucking close to the finish line.

"I've been thinking about that. Is it so important we marry tomorrow?"

I'm insanely triggered by her question, and I pin her to the bed, straddling her body. "What did I say about a foregone conclusion?"

"Is tomorrow some important holiday or something?" she asks. I'm still not liking where this questioning is going. This woman's trying to test me, so I should fuck her right now, making sure she marries me as soon as humanly possible.

"No, but I'm not waiting any longer."

She smiles and rolls her eyes at me. "I didn't say wait longer. I was thinking...well, I thought maybe it was best if we could just get married today with our family already here."

"Really? You don't really want all eyes on you?" I don't want anyone's eyes on my bride, especially male eyes.

"After last night, I don't think it matters to me. With the house a mess, the wedding reception can't be there. Besides, you've just had men die, and I don't think it's right celebrating with such a grand event like that."

"That's true. If you're sure, I'll talk to your parents."

"I'm positive."

I stare at her in amazement. Not only does she want to marry me sooner, but she doesn't want the big hoopla that's already been planned because of the deaths last night. "You're going to be a great queen at my side." I kiss her slowly, pulling back to look at her gorgeous face.

"Thank you."

"Let's get dressed so we can deal with all of this. Your father and mother already have a lot to worry about at the house. I'm sure there's water damage."

"Okay. Well, you have to let me go so we can do it." All I want to do is fuck her, but she's right.

"I love having you under me," I admit. I love more than just that. Everything about Aria proves more and more that she was made just for me.

"Just think—after it's all over today, you can have your way with me; otherwise, we'll have to wait until tomorrow."

"Very excellent point." I press my lips to hers once and then pop off the bed. She sits up and scoots off, looking sexy as hell in that nightie. I need to buy her mother a huge gift for that one. I'm guessing she wants a lot more grandbabies. I bite back a groan and adjust my throbbing rod. What I need is a cold shower, although I don't think that will do much good because just thinking about Aria stiffens me up.

"Staring at my ass isn't going to get you dressed any faster." She's a bad girl for sure, enjoying every second of my torture. I'll return the favor later.

"I'm going to make you pay for it later, bella. Go get dressed so I don't bend you over." I walk to the closet and pull out a freshly cleaned suit while she saunters past me to her side, looking through the pretty sundresses.

I quickly exit before I see what she selects. I don't need any more temptation, and Aria is my sole temptress, beckoning me without even being aware of the impact she has on men. I've glared at and threatened many men over the past two years.

Slipping into the bathroom, I shower and get ready. By the time I step out, Aria's sitting on the bed, looking gorgeous in her pale blue flowery sundress that hugs her ample chest and shows off her slender shoulders that I ache to bite.

"You look beautiful, Aria. As always, of course. Let us go down to the kitchen for some breakfast, and then we can talk to your parents and mine." She nods, and I take her hand, leading us downstairs. Several of my men are stationed around the house, each of them keeping their eyes to the ground when my wife passes. I've warned every single one of them that she's my queen and demands the utmost respect and protection.

"Good morning, Dom," Nero says. "Good morning, Mrs. Bianchi."

"Aria, amore, this is my second-in-command and cousin, Nero Bianchi."

"Hello, Nero, and it's Aria." He looks to me for approval with her name.

"Seeing that he's my cousin, it's okay for him to call you Aria. The rest of my men will address you as Mrs. Bianchi."

"Even though we're not...."

"Woman, I swear you're asking for me to redden that ass of yours."

"I'm pretty sure I've flat-out put it on you, but nothing," she huffs.

"Only a few more hours."

"It's twenty-six hours, to be exact," Nero adds.

"Actually, that's something I plan to change. No discussion, and we need to speak to our parents, but we are going to cancel the wedding. My queen doesn't think it's in good taste to continue with an elaborate celebration at this time."

"Smart. Should I send out the notifications? I've actually been contacted by many of the families, and they send their condolences about the bombing and deaths. They've asked about the wedding, but I had no information on that."

"Inform them it's canceled due to the circumstances." He nods and walks away.

"Come on, and let's break the news to our parents who are anxious to throw a true Italian wedding." She rolls her eyes and shakes her head. I can't blame them, though; I wanted it special for Aria as well.

"There you two are," my mother says, coming up to us for a hug.

"Sweetie, we've been talking about the wedding. It's not like we can have it at our estate tomorrow."

"Actually, Domani and I wanted to talk about that. With everything going on and the loss of his men, we believe that we should cancel the wedding and reception."

"Whoa..."

"No, she's still marrying me, but we think it should be super private—and today."

"Is that what you want, piccolina?"

"Yes, Papa. It was my idea."

"Well, we could do it, but what of all the guests?"

"The fire has already had the phones ringing off the hook, so we notify them that it's been postponed. Besides, we could still have people coming after us."

The rest of the morning, Aria and I part to get a lot more work done. If she's around me, all I want to do is hold and kiss her. My brother and cousin will stand in as my best men while our staff watch us marry on our grand staircase. By the end of the morning, every guest has been contacted and informed that nothing has been scheduled due to the unfortunate events. They all understand, but many wondered why I don't still just marry her. Aria Grasso is an heiress, and there could have been plenty of suitors if I hadn't made it clear that I'd shoot anyone in the other families if they approached her father for a deal. I informed everyone there would be a war.

Over the years, I'd been asked if I'd changed my mind, but I responded with, "Would you like a bullet in the head?"

A knock on my office door brings my attention up from my notes. "Son, are you ready?"

"You know it. Is Father Falcone here?"

"Yes, he just arrived as well as the construction crew to evaluate the front gate and guard shack."

"Okay. I'll talk to the construction crew, and then we should be ready to marry in ten minutes." My hands are shaking as I adjust my suit.

"Are you okay?"

"Anxious. I've waited so long for this day."

"I know."

"Maybe we should have the construction crew wait."

"No, I want all my attention devoted to Aria the second we say our vows."

It doesn't take long to meet with the foreman assigned to the project. He knows who I am and that I won't tolerate a shitty job or delays. I dismiss them and head back inside to get the formalities over with.

The front of the house has been arranged nicely with seating and flowers from my mother's private rose garden. Photos are being taken by Luigi, who has a knack for photography. I anxiously wait at the bottom of the steps. As the music begins to play, Aria appears at the top of the steps with her father bringing her to me. God, she looks like an angel. Her long black hair has been curled and is splayed over her bare shoulders. Her gown is elegant as it flows around her with tiny crystals shining radiantly on the bell of the dress. Although it's not far down the stairs, it feels like an eternity. I lose my patience and take a step forward, but then Nero grips my shoulder and whispers, "Relax. The wait is almost over."

A smile spreads over her face, and that's the first time that I can see that she's added some makeup, accentuating her already flawless features. When they finally reach the bottom step, her father generously puts her hand into mine without waiting for the father to ask. "Today, we unite families, and I am grateful to have two sons-in-law that love my girls." He kisses her cheek and moves back to his wife, who is shedding a tear or two. I steal a glance at my mother, and she's a mess as well. I'm happier than anything in the world. "He's right, my queen. I love you more than words can say."

I turn to the priest and have him begin. The second he declares us man and wife, I pull her close, sliding my hand into her curls and dropping my mouth onto hers with a kiss so possessive it takes a clearing of Nero's throat to remind me that I'm in front of a priest.

"May I present Mr. And Mrs. Domani Bianchi."

"Congratulations," everyone cheers.

I bring her hand to my lips and kiss the backside. "Thank you, my queen."

"That's Mrs. Bianchi to you," she hisses, running her fingers under my suit jacket and up around my neck. "I want another kiss, Domani."

"Excuse us for a moment."

"We're preparing lunch. It should be ready in twenty.

Don't be consummating anything right now," my mother huffs.

"Yes, Mama. I just need to have a word alone with my bride."

I drag her down the hall to my office. As soon as I have the door closed, I have her back against the door. "Mrs. Bianchi, I think it's time to reward us both for being such a good girl." I kiss her hard as fuck as I work my suit jacket off me.

I drop to the floor and lift up her dress, sliding under and parting her thighs. Her panties are drenched, clinging to her mound. I slide them off and tuck them in my pocket. I part her lower lips and swipe my tongue along her seam. She cries out, slapping her hand to her mouth. Slipping out from underneath, I move her to my desk and sit her on the surface, tossing her dress over her middle so I can get a proper angle on her heat. Fuck, she's so sweet. I didn't know what to expect, but I've found that she'll be my best breakfast every single morning. My fingers creep up her thighs until I'm pushing the first one into her pussy. She's so hot and tight that I'm going to come in my pants. Running my finger in and out, I coax moans from her throat, licking between deep strokes. Her womb needs to open for me, but we don't have time. For now, I'm going to make her cream all over my face.

She lifts one hand off the desk and thrusts it into my hair, tugging me closer, rubbing my face in her sweetness. I swipe quick, staccato movements with my tongue, feeling her body locking up.

"Give it to me, amore mia. Come for me."

She bites on the cloth of her gown, muffling her orgasm. I drink her release, licking her slit until she calms down.

Standing, I adjust her dress. "Such a good girl. You're going to feed your husband every day, aren't you?"

"Even if I'm not a good girl?"

"That works for me."

"What about your needs?" she asks, moving to lower herself off the desk.

Shaking my head, I look into her eyes. "You've given me what I needed when you took my name. Besides, I'd hate to ruin your dress."

"I suppose that wouldn't be a good look."

"No. I need to wash up so your father doesn't want to shoot me, knowing that I've been eating his daughter out."

"Yeah. Although I wonder if my cries were heard."

"This room is soundproof, just in case there are eager ears," I mutter, standing inside my bathroom with the door open.

"Oh. That's good." The tenor in her voice makes me suspicious. I finish scrubbing my face and brushing my hair, and then I move toward her, tossing the towel back in the bathroom.

Her mood instantly sours. "Whatever thought is going through your head, I don't bring women to my home. It's just for business meetings."

"So you have a place for the other women," she mutters under her breath. I get it. She's insecure—jealous. I invade her space, pin her to the desk as I cup her face. "There's no one else. There has never been another woman. I've been faithful to you long before I knew you existed. The day your presence was known to me, I knew that I could never betray you."

"Wait. Are you telling me..."

"Yes, cara mia. The head of the Bianchi Family is a virgin."

"It's hard to fathom."

"Not as hard as it was as a teen boy."

"I bet. Your hormones must have been going insane."

"Yeah, I let it influence my attitude, and I worked alongside Nero as the muscle. It's not like I had any particular chick of interest, but I was growing and growing, needing that release. We went to strip clubs to claim our money, and motherfuckers were getting more than just a lap dance, and I got curious. I mentioned it to my father, and he said he'd lock my ass in the house. He didn't want me to soil the Bianchi bloodline with putanas."

"They're a dime a dozen in our world because there are men willing to take what they have to offer."

"Yes. Most don't know that about me."

"But you knew what to do...when you were...." She becomes silent, nervous as a blush covers her cheeks.

Cupping her face, I look into her amber-colored eyes and explain, "I listened to the aria your body was performing for me. Every little moan, sigh, or vibrating thighs told me what I was doing. I'm a quick learner, it seems."

"Or it's that I was super horny."

Damned brat. My cock throbs with need to show her how much I'd love her to be horny twenty-four seven. "Could be. We'll have to research it later. Now that I've spilled my guts like a man with a knife at his throat, maybe we should join your family."

"Sounds like a good idea." I help her off the desk and then I go into the drawer. Sweetie, this is something I forgot to give you. I'll leave it in here, but it's the cards and money you'll need as my wife along with a new cell phone."

"Oh, wow—thank you!" She grabs the phone, and the home screen is the one I have on mine. It's of her sleeping in my arms. "Ah, this is so perfect. I can't believe you did this, Domani."

"I'd do anything for you." Spearing my hands into her hair, I kiss her hard, slipping my tongue into her mouth, silently telling her how fucking serious I am. She moans, wrapping her legs around my waist firmly, grinding her kitty on my shaft through the many layers between us. I pin her back down on the desk, aching as we rut and rock against each other, lust shooting through us. I'm about to come and I drag my mouth lower, tugging her gown down enough to get one of her tits in my mouth. She cries out, and I capture her lips again.

A hard rap on the door pulls our attention away. "Yes," I snarl, straightening up to a standing position and helping Aria fix her top.

"Lovebirds, they sent me to fetch you. Don't kill the messenger," Nero says. I want to choke him right now. My dick is so hard it could break off. I was just about to nut, and I'm betting Aria was too.

"We're on our way." A minute later, when we're semi-presentable, I open the door with anger plastered all over my face, but my sweet Aria squeals, rushing to Nero with her phone in his face. "Look at the adorable picture he put on my phone."

Nero and I chuckle as he gently moves the phone out of his face. "It's the same one he has on his."

She whips her head back at me with her mouth open. I just shrug. I have nothing to hide when it comes to my attraction to my wife. Well, I have some things to hide, but I don't think she's ready to know how deep my obsession goes. "What can I say? I love having you as mine."

"Same here," she says, kissing my cheek before hurrying to everyone else.

Nero grabs my hand and shakes it. "Congrats, Dom. She's perfect for you."

"I know." There's a sense of peace that fills me now that she's my wife.

"Come on, Giuseppe made a huge lunch."

"I'm not even hungry."

"Not for food. Soon, after lunch, sneak her ass to bed."

"If I do, you won't see me for the rest of the day until tomorrow. I've waited too long for her."

"I bet. I don't have an obsession, but I've stuck to your father's edict as well. Bianchi blood runs deep. I'm waiting for my future bride. It's a pity that I haven't found her yet."

"You will one day."

7

Aria

I HEAD into the dining room with a smile on my face. I'm so happy that it's hard to even explain. Domani is crazy about me. When I open the door, I'm surprised by the extravagant display. "Where's Domani?"

"He's coming right behind me."

"Wow, this is so beautiful." There are flowers from the wedding around the room in large bouquets, and along two walls are large tables covered with white tablecloths and a full array of food in a magnificent display.

Hands slide around my waist and I smile, tilting my head back as Domani kisses the crown of my head. "Will this do, my queen?"

"It's wonderful."

"Everyone." The room becomes silent at my husband's voice. "Thank you for putting this together for my bride and myself with little to no time. I am grateful and pleased to present my queen, my wife, Aria Bianchi." The family and staff clap loudly as Nero whistles and Luigi snaps pictures.

My attention is drawn to the other door as it opens, and our chef comes in with another cart. On it is a beautiful three-layer cake. It's not the wedding cake we ordered, but it's still incredible.

Domani helps me to my seat, pushing my chair in and kissing my cheek before taking the seat next to me. "Congratulations to you both! Cheers to the power couple!" Everyone cheers.

"Thank you. Please, let us eat before our food grows cold." Domani and I are the first to be served and then the rest follow. The waitstaff depart as we enjoy our meal as if it's just another family Sunday dinner.

"So, Niccolò, I don't know much about you, but it's nice to finally meet you," I say, finally speaking to my brother-in-law for the first time. Just like Nero, Niccolò looks so much like Domani. They are all handsome. While they are all over six feet tall, Niccolò has more of a runner's build. The other two look more intimidating. Nero's enormous, but it's the power in Domani's carriage that makes him appear the fiercest. It turns me on so much to be the wife of an animal in a gentleman's suit.

"Sorry, Aria. I should have been here sooner. I'm glad I didn't miss the wedding."

"I'm pleased that you could make it, brother." Domani smiles at his brother who looks like he's concerned about something. The slight upturn of Domani's lips seems to settle him. Could he be afraid of his brother? No? Maybe of disappointing him. That's definitely something I could see. Niccolò hardly speaks unless spoken to throughout the meal as the rest of the family talk about all matters.

As lunch wraps up, the staff come in to clean, and we stand to cut our cake. Our hands touch, slicing through the cake, and my pulse amplifies like lightning has struck, but it's just his hand on mine. "I can't wait until my hands are all over you, amore mia."

"Neither can I." I kiss his cheek, and suddenly he releases the cake knife and sets it on the table. Cupping my face, he drops his mouth down on mine, returning my innocent kiss with one of pure need. His fingers dig into my hair until he's gripping the base of my skull. I can't stop from throwing my arms around his neck, teasing the tips of his hair.

Cheers erupt around the room. "I expect we'll be having some grandbabies within the year," his mother says.

"Can we have some cake before you two get started?" my father remarks, causing me to blush and release my hold on Domani. He does the same, but the smile on his face says more than words can. It's a promise that we'll finish what we started soon. The staff serves the slices, while Domani hands me mine. We share a piece, feeding each other. I can't eat another bite, so we make small talk when all I want to do is have my husband work my body out over and over again.

Needing to think of something else, I address Giuseppe who comes to take the cake back to be refrigerated. "Did you make this, Giuseppe?" Giuseppe and his assistants worked miracles on our meal.

"Yes, Mrs. Bianchi. Was it to your liking?" I can see the pride the man has about every meal he prepares. It's clearly something that makes him smile.

"Thank you, Giuseppe. Everything has been perfectly delicious. And the cake—it's incredible, and so much more than necessary."

"Nonsense, you deserve the cake of a queen, but we must settle for this one." He frowns, as if this cake wasn't fantastic. Yes, it's not as intricate or lavish and much smaller than the one I wanted, but he had hours to make it, not two weeks. It's a miracle I got this beauty, and I'm pleased most thoroughly with the care he took in making it.

"Although I believe no one should disagree with my bride, I have to side with Giuseppe. I'm sorry that you weren't given the wedding you should have had." Domani caresses my cheek.

"Yes, we had a larger wedding for my driver and his wife," Cormack says.

"Still, I'm pleased. Now, enough. I'm happy, and I'd love to change out of this gown because I'm so stuffed," I say, pushing my chair back and standing up. I'll take whatever excuse I can to get a moment alone with Domani.

Domani stands with me. "Goodnight everyone. Giuseppe, bring dinner up at nine."

"Yes, Mr. Bianchi."

"What? It's only four," I mutter as Domani leads me to the door.

"Wife, I've been more than generous with sharing you with our families." He flips me over his shoulder. "We'll see everyone at breakfast." My brute of a husband carries me out of the dining room and upstairs.

"Um...I just ate."

"Oh. Sorry, amore." He sets me on my feet as we reach the top of the stairs.

"It's fine, but being upside down, I need a moment." I press my hand up to calm the tension coming from him.

"Are you well?" He cups my face tenderly, lifting my face to meet his gaze. The simple act heats up my entire body.

Smiling up at him, I nod. "Yes. I'm fine. Just a little full."

"You're about to be a lot full, but first, let me get you in our room to relax." He wags his brows, making me giggle. I'm not as full as I'm playing at and suddenly, my stomach is fluttering for another reason. I'm nervous and excited about becoming his in every way tonight. All throughout lunch, I replayed what he said in my head. We're on a level playing field.

Taking a deep breath, I enter our bedroom to see red rose petals leading to the bathroom and the bed. "Wow, you still made it so special."

"It's just a day early. I've been waiting for this moment for far too long." He pulls me into his arms, gently kisses my lips, and then slides his mouth down to my neck, swiping his tongue along my pulse. Tilting my head, I give him more room as I cling to his biceps. Goodness, I'm in heaven and we've only gotten started.

"Come, let me undress you," he whispers. I spin in his arms and then feel his knuckles lightly graze my bare back before reaching the zipper. He tugs the zipper down, which quickly gives way. With a slight wiggle, my gown cascades to the floor in a pool of gauzy material. Domani takes my hand as I step out of the white puddle, leaving me in just a pair of panties and my kitten heels. As he stands behind me, Domani grips my long hair in one hand, tilting my head to the side before he slowly brushes open-mouthed kisses along my jaw and down to my neck. "My wife, my queen. Mine," he whispers reverently before nipping on my earlobe.

I lean back, resting on his broad chest, letting him feel his way all over my flesh and lighting up every nerve ending. He makes me feel so delicate, feminine, and safe as his fingers skim over my arms to my breasts. The feel of his hands cupping them, plucking lightly on my nipples, shatters any inhibitions. I moan with each squeeze, caress, and I need more. "Domani." I don't even recognize the whimper that crosses my lips. My longing is so real, so intense that I can't stop the sounds coming from me.

"You're so beautiful, Aria." He spins me around and scoops me up in his arms, carrying me to our bed and laying me down with tender care. Tugging his tie loose, he tosses it onto the chair and then methodically he removes his clothes until he's standing in front of me in just his black silk boxers covering his impressive length.

"Wow," I murmur, staring at his impressive package.

"Thank you, Aria." Climbing onto the bed, he straddles my body and brings his mouth to mine as we begin to kiss. No dreams, no fantasies have prepared me for this moment —the way his body presses into mine without squishing me, and the way his tongue slides down my torso.

"Domani."

"Relax. I want to taste my wife's pussy before I stretch out her perfectly tight core, filling her with my sons," he commands and my body responds, gushing between my thighs as I open for him. He slinks down, grabbing the hem of my panties and yanks, tearing them from my body. He wastes no time getting down on his stomach as he swipes his tongue along my slit. My breath catches as pleasure shoots through me. His deft fingers tease my opening, pushing one digit inside me and testing my ability to stay in control. My hands dig into the mattress, clutching the sheets.

"That's it, baby. Come for me."

"Domani, don't stop."

"Never." I cry out, gripping his head with my thighs as I come on his tongue and fingers. He pumps into me as I squirt all over his face. Licking me once more, he pulls back and slides his boxers off, freeing that huge cock of his. I want it in me, but I'm not sure it's gonna fit.

He kisses his way up my body until the tip is at my entrance. I take a deep breath before he pushes into me and then through my innocence. I cry out, feeling the burning stretch until his mouth claims mine. A moan slips out as I adjust. "Sorry, my queen. It will be over soon."

"It's getting better. You're just so big."

He chuckles and smiles. "Thank you." We kiss as he moves slowly in and out. Finally the pain passes, and pleasure replaces it. "God, you're so damn beautiful."

I marvel at his handsome, muscular build, raking my nails over his biceps as he takes me, owns me. The sensation of being his fills me up as we both come. Domani clings to me, wrapping me up in his arms, and he flips onto his back so I rest on his broad chest where his heart beats out of control.

I thought I loved him before, but now I'm sure I'm in real danger of him destroying my heart.

---

*W*e've been married a full week and I find myself always wanting to hunt my husband down and kiss his lips. That's why I'm now sitting in the library reading a book, or at least trying to. I was supposed to help my mom sort through my things, but I kept getting distracted, so she sent me away and went to have tea with Mrs. Bianchi. I put down the book because it does no good when all I can do is think about Domani. I'm always thinking about him, which makes me pretty pathetic. I've been fascinated since the day in the limo, and now I'm his bride. One he's already killed for. Franco died because he wanted me to the point of attacking the Bianchi Family.

What I don't understand is why Franco had to do what he did? I hardly knew him, and I never felt any feelings toward anyone but Domani.

I gasp. "Domani broke his arm." All those years ago, it was Domani who taught him a lesson. One he refused to learn. But why was Domani the one to do that?

Rushing out of the library, needing answers, I nearly collide with my father. "Sweetheart, is something wrong?"

"Yes. Why did Domani break Franco's arm in the first place?"

"Because he tried to kiss you."

"No. I mean why would Domani be involved in that incident when we were only promised to each other less than a month ago? And don't lie to me."

"He wanted you protected from the day he requested to marry you."

"Day he requested...that was weeks ago." Even as I say it, I know it's not the case. My father can't hide the truth in his eyes. "He's the reason I never got to enjoy hanging out with friends and why I had to be homeschooled. He wanted me isolated."

Angry, I try to storm away, but my dad grabs my arm, stopping me. "Wait. We need to talk, Aria."

"Two years too late. Excuse me." He lets go of my arm, and I head in to find my husband. My blood boils with every step closer. I point to my guard and snarl, "Don't follow me." She backs up and stays put.

8

Domani

IT'S BEEN a week since we married, and I can't express how happy this woman has made me. I'd planned a honeymoon for us, but with the deaths of my men, Aria demanded we cancel it. She has been a pillar of strength when it comes to handling the arrangements, making sure our men get their proper burials and their families are well taken care of.

I knew she had it in her to be amazing. Everything about Aria makes me fucking happy, and the sex has been incredible and often to the point that I'm sure her pussy has to be sore from how often I'm balls deep in her. What I wouldn't give to get away just the two of us somewhere secluded where I can spend days worshipping her and spoiling her with no eyes lurking around.

Her parents are supposed to be leaving soon to go back to their home, but the rebuild will take another week. It's hard to feel guilty when we come out of a room looking thoroughly fucked and her parents are around. If they don't like it, they need to book a hotel somewhere because I can't get enough of my bride.

Just sitting here thinking about her makes my balls feel heavy again, like I need to drain them in my queen, but we just went at it for hours early this morning. It's insane how insatiable we are. I adjust my cock because it's hard to sit like this, but I have to get my ass together. Not everything is about needing Aria naked.

A knock at my office door takes me by surprise because Aria's with her mother as they sort through Aria's things that have been brought from her parents' estate. "Enter."

"Domani. I need to speak with you." That isn't the tone I like to hear from her. It's cold, almost indifferent. Nothing like the woman I was just daydreaming about.

"Yes, wife, but you know you never have to knock in this home. It's yours," I remind her.

A big mistake. Her eyes flare at me with an untold anger that concerns me, and then she lets me have it. "Don't tell me what to do, damn it." She shakes her head, chest heaving as she returns her glare straight at me. "I've just learned that you're the reason that I've been locked away for two years. I can't believe you did that. What—were you afraid I'd find someone else before I reached eighteen? That I'd be spoiled?"

In a flash, I step around the desk to try to calm her down. Just as I close the distance, her hand comes swiftly across my face. I grip it, absorbing the sting for the cheap shot that it was. "Wife. I will never lay a hand on you, but you will treat me with the same decency," I grit out, pinning her ass to the edge of my desk with my body pressed firmly against hers.

"I don't owe you any decency. I can't believe you." She yanks her hand from my grip, and I let it go because I don't want her to hurt herself. When she heads for the door, I cuff her waist and lift her off her feet. "Put me down, you monster. I hate you." I hear the tears in her voice, and I do feel like a fucking monster.

Setting her back on her feet, I hold her and lean in. "I didn't lock you up. The day I made you mine, you became my weak spot."

"Let me go. You disgust me." She tosses her head back, nearly full-on headbutting me, but hits just my cheek. I let her go because for a moment I'm too damn heated to speak rationally to her. She darts out from the room like she's afraid I'm going to give chase. Right now, I want as much distance as possible between us, and yet no distance at the same time.

I'm not going to chase after her because I don't know how to fix this. She can't leave the house anyway, so I have some time to figure out how to make it right. I slam my office door closed to avoid anyone coming to see what's wrong. I walk over to my cabinet and pour myself a tumbler full of bourbon and drink the entire thing. I take a look in the mirror, and it looks like my little spitfire of a wife left a nice fucking bruise on my cheek. I sit down on my leather sofa off to the side with a fresh glass of bourbon and close my eyes.

There's a knock at my door. "Go away."

"Domani, can I speak to you for a moment?" my father-in-law asks through the door.

"I'm not in the mood to talk, so go away," I snarl.

"This is about Aria," he pleads.

I want to bite his head off right fucking now, but I relent. "Come in."

"I came in to apologize. It's my fault. She learned that all the other families were supposed to stay away from her. I didn't tell her about the abduction attempt."

"What? I don't know how to fix this. She hates me."

"No, she doesn't. She's upset, but she loves you." I doubt it, shaking my head. We've only been together a short time, but she made it clear that I haven't gotten any closer to winning her heart; in fact, I think I've done the opposite. Orgasms aren't the only thing I want from her, and she proved that she doesn't want anything from me. "She's young, Domani. Hot-headed and hurt. She's pissed at me as well, but I'm sure she'll understand when you finally get her to sit down and listen. Aria's always been the bullheaded one. It's one of the reasons I made the deal with you and agreed to keep it a secret. If she knew then, she might have done something stupid to get out of it and likely put herself in danger."

I could see that happening only in his head because I'd never have let her sneak away. My men were doing their job incredibly well by averting several attempts on her, and she didn't even know it. I had my eyes on her nearly all hours of the day, either in person or via surveillance systems. My obsession with Aria was sick and twisted to the point that I learned everything I could about her. "I need to find her and fix this. Even if I have to tie her down to get her to listen."

"Ties work well, and they're less likely to leave any markings," he says. He turns back and adds, "She's gone into your mother's garden." He leaves the door open after he walks out, tempting me to go after my wife.

I really have to make this right between us. The longer it festers, the more damage will be done. I swing around my desk and close down my computer. I'm just about to walk out the door when my phone rings, and I scoop it off the desk. I find the silent alarm has been tripped by Luigi.

He calls me. "Domani, they've taken Aria."

"Who took her?" I snarl, running out of my office and out to the front of the house.

"Her guards," Luigi says.

"What? Her guards?" Aria only has one guard around the house that's actually assigned to her since John disappeared.

"Yeah, her guards. John's back, and he had her guard, Torres, with them as Aria got into the car."

"They're dead. We need to get my wife back now." I'm seeing red as we watch the surveillance video. I load up her phone tracking, but it shows the phone's here in the house. "Fuck. She doesn't have her phone." Then I remember. "Her ring. Please tell me she didn't take it off." I pull up the trace on her ring and get a steady ping of it flying down the expressway. My men and I hop in several vehicles, many with hidden gun compartments. We give chase at a distance because I don't want to give them any excuse to harm her. My men scope out the vehicle and report that they can't see Aria, so she must be in the trunk or the back seat, which means they've taken her against her will. It's a bit of a relief that she didn't voluntarily leave me, but I can't stop the dread that's filling me.

"They're exiting on the ramp that leads to an airfield," one of my men says through our walkies.

"We need a plan. I don't want any plane taking off before we find her. There's no way I'm letting her get in the air. Understood?" I call out to my men on the walkies.

"Got it. I have a friend who works there. We'll call in an issue."

"Good. Stall."

How did John get access to a plane to kidnap my wife? We've had no information on the fucker for weeks. His bank and apartment haven't been touched since the day he disappeared. Torres has had a clean record working with the family for three years and never showed any signs of betrayal. I'm gonna string them up and torture them when I get my hands on them.

I silently pray that Aria is okay.

9

Aria

I DASH into the back rose garden, blinded with tears until I run into a wall. I look up, knowing it's probably one of Domani's guards, but instantly I know I'm wrong because he hasn't let go. Domani's men know not to put their hands on me at all or they'll be cut off.

Hesitantly peering upward, I see it's my old guard, John. "John, what are you doing here?" I'm pleasantly surprised to see he's not dead.

"They didn't tell you I'm back?" He cocks his brow up, his lips firmly closed shut.

"No. I mean, well, he doesn't tell me a lot," I mutter, covering my mouth immediately. It's not proper to share our business with others, no matter how mad I am at Domani. "I shouldn't have said that."

"I won't say anything. Well, I'm surprised that you actually married. I only learned of it today," he grumbles as if he's bothered.

"Why are you surprised? It was scheduled to happen for

a long time." Suddenly, I don't feel so happy to see my old guard. There's something different about his tone and stance. It's not friendly in the least.

"Because I thought he'd been killed," he snarls. I take a step backward, hoping to create some distance. I don't hear anyone else nearby, which is expected since Domani's men don't usually follow me like hound dogs. Even my guard is pretty lax with my protection inside the house. It's what I prefer, but I'm regretting that choice at the moment.

"Where have you been, John?" I challenge, saying it loud so someone can hear me.

"Waiting for you." He grips my arm roughly, spinning my back to his front and pulling me close to him.

"Let me go," I command, but he doesn't. I try to kick him as I go to scream, but his hand comes over my mouth. Suddenly, I lose consciousness. "Domani," I sigh as everything goes dark.

"This bitch better not die. I want her to make it until I get my money," Torres complains. She's in on it too? Who are they working for, and where are they taking me? I keep my eyes closed even though my ears are open. Fuck, my head's still spinning. What did he give me? We hit a bump, and I swallow the groan. I need to find a way to get out of this vehicle, but I can feel we're moving at a high rate of speed.

"Do you think he's going to pay us even though she's used goods?" he asks. Fuck that prick.

"He wants her anyway, even if she's ruined." I wish I carried a gun because I could save myself. Hell, it would have been wise to have my phone on me, but no—I had to throw it at the wall, smashing it.

"She's married to him, though," John sounds so fucking disgusted by that fact. "He doesn't know that she fucking masturbated with Bianchi's name on her lips. No one knows. Even Bianchi with his cameras in her room didn't know it," John remarks with a chuckle. I didn't realize he could hear me. I hold back a gasp. God, Domani has no boundaries.

"How could he not know if he has cameras in there?" That's something I want to know as well.

"Because he didn't install them until recently, and as if she knew, she didn't call out his name anymore."

"Well, that's only a problem until Domani Bianchi is dead—which is only a matter of time." God, I want to rip her hair out and beat her to death. If I make it out of this alive, heads will roll. I may lose the love of my life because he hates me, but I'll never be anyone's victim.

"Yeah, he's going to kill anyone who gets in his way," John adds, sending chills through my body.

"This guy is nuts," Torres says, sounding nervous about whoever is paying them.

"That he is, but he's paying us a fortune and we can skip town after." Who would pay a fortune for me? I'm hot, but not like insanely beautiful to the point that someone would go through all this. Hell, this is the second motherfucker in a week to risk his life to steal me from Domani.

"Let's get her to him and get our money, babe." So they're a couple.

The vehicle comes to a stop, and John cuts the engine. I pretend to be still out cold when the back door opens and John lifts me over his shoulder. I feel the wind on my face as if we're in a field or something. Then I hear a plane flying extremely close. Shit. Are we at an airport? I don't know how long I was out, so I can't even guess which airport they took me to. Damn it.

We're still on the ground, but now the wind has stopped.

"You've got her. Why the fuck is she unconscious?" The voice echoes, making me guess we're in a hangar. "She better be okay." I know that deep Irish accent anywhere. Fuck, it's Peter Delaney, Cormack's brother.

"She started to scream so we gave her the dose you told us to use," John explains.

"Damn it, my sweet girl, I'll take care of you."

"Where's our money? We need to skip town before the Bianchis find us." The two shots startle me. I see and hear their bodies fall. Several other sets of footsteps shuffle into action.

"So you are now awake, my beauty. I took out the trash. You can't hire good help. Let me get you inside." He has a freakishly strong grip on me as I try to push out of his arms.

"What are you doing? Why?" I question, looking up at the scary brute.

"You should have been mine. I've been trying for two years to claim you, but they kept you well protected. It only took the right people willing to turn on your father and that fucking scum you married. I know you didn't have a choice, so I forgive you for your infidelity, but don't think I'll let you whore around on me again." I shiver internally as I fight the revulsion building in me.

"I don't know what you're talking about, Peter. You and I were never meant to be together," I say as if that's going to make him see reason.

"I've been trying to get with you since we met in Ireland, but I had a wife to dispose of. Then, that piece of shit made an agreement with your father. I tried to take you once, but that didn't work out and I was almost caught. It seems you're a man-eater, Aria, my sweet. Several men have died trying to take you. However, this time I've got you, and they can't get you back."

He sits me in a seat across from him as he sits closer to the door. I watch it, judging my chances at making a run for it. "Relax—our flight leaves in a bit."

"Oh goodness." My mind goes straight to Domani and the look on his face when I left him. I hurt him, told him I hated him...and I may never see him again. He'll be killed because of me. I was locked away to protect me from men like Peter. "Peter, can we talk about this?"

"About what, my sweet Aria?"

"I'm married already. Why do you want me anyway? We haven't spoken since Gloria and Cormack's wedding."

"Yes, because they kept me from you."

"Kept you away? You're related to my brother-in-law."

"Yes, but no man was allowed to get close."

"I don't understand why you didn't try to visit us as a member of your brother's family. It wouldn't have been hard. You must not care that much about me if you were willing to stay away."

"Hardly. I blame my brother for not fighting for my VISA to America."

"How did you get here?"

"I have friends that made it happen. Did you miss me?"

"I don't even know you."

"You will in good time, and I'll be a much better husband than that fuck. He doesn't know how to treat a woman well." I do my best to hold my tongue. He got rid of his wife so he could pursue me; he's terrible when it comes to women.

"What's taking so long?" he shouts over his shoulder.

The pilot answers via the plane intercom, "Sir, we are delayed due to some inclement weather. We need another hour before we can fly."

"Fine. Let me know if we can depart sooner." He turns his attention to me and then says, "It's fine. Those fools don't even know I have you. They think those rotting corpses stole you. We have time to relax. Would you care for something to drink?"

"No. Thank you," I bite out. I don't trust him at all.

"You must be thirsty," he insists, which worries me even more.

"Yes. I'm parched, but I can't be sure you won't drug me."

"How could you think such a thing? I want to make you my wife. I'd never hurt you."

"But I was drugged earlier," I express, leaving out the fact that he killed his last wife.

"Please bring my bride a bottle of water, sealed," he shouts instead of using the damned intercom. Goodness, was he born in a barn or something? No manners whatsoever.

"I'm sleepy. Is there somewhere I can rest until we take off?"

"The seats recline. Please take advantage of that because at this moment, it's all I can trust you with. I need you in my sight at all times unless you want to be tied up." I'm gonna stab him in the eye one day for sure.

"No. I'll sit here. Okay." I sit down and press the button, lowering the headrest, and close my eyes. I can't handle looking at him and pretending not to be disgusted. He repulses me more and more with every second that ticks by. I found him slimy and creepy when we first met as he stared at me with his wife by his side. He's the epitome of super insane. My sister was afraid to be alone with him, although

Cormack never let that happen because he didn't trust his filthy brother either.

All I can hope for is that Domani can find me even though I've given him no reason to want to. I was a total bitch, even striking him. If I could change everything I said, I would. "Madam, here is your drink." I open my eyes and take the bottle from the flight attendant. Why would they have a glass bottle of water instead of plastic? It seems like an expensive waste, but more power to Evian for selling me a weapon.

My mind goes to ways to break free from this asshole. As I open the bottle, I hear a shot go off and the attendant screams. Did he shoot her too? I close the cap on my water bottle, hoping I don't incur his wrath.

"Aria." I turn my eyes to the entrance, and there's my husband standing there with his gun trained on Peter, who's bleeding from this leg.

"Domani," I gasp, feeling lightheaded from happiness, but then a sense of fearlessness hits me. I stand, moving toward my husband. Sensing Peter's movements, I swing the glass bottle and crack it across his head. Peter looks at me with pure betrayal as he loses consciousness. Nero comes from behind Domani with two more guards. Domani yanks Peter's gun away before zip-tying him.

"Aria, that's my queen. Come here." He pulls me into his arms, not waiting for me to cross the short distance. "I'll be dealing with him later, but I need to get Aria home."

He carries me over his shoulder and down the plane stairs. I don't know what to say since I was so mean to him, saying things in anger and striking him. What if he doesn't forgive me? He sets me down and helps me into the back seat of his SUV without a word.

And it stays that way—the road back home is full of

silence. I'm scared to speak first, so I don't speak at all, finding the window much more interesting. He only speaks to his driver, and then his phone rings. "We'll be there in two minutes. Your daughter is with me," he snarls into the phone before hanging up.

Your daughter? He didn't refer to me as his wife at all. I sit back and look out the window, seeing nothing but my own devastation peering back at me. It feels like the longest ride in history as the silence screams between us.

As soon as we reach the estate, my parents pull me into their arms, hugging me like crazy. "She needs to get to bed and have a doctor examine her," Domani informs my parents, tugging me away from them.

"I'm fine. I don't need a doctor. He didn't hurt me."

"Very well. Still, it's time for bed." He walks me up to the bedroom we share and says, "Take a shower and get some sleep." He leaves me standing there with my mouth open and heart crumbling like I deserve.

10

Domani

I WALK her to our bedroom and leave. Watching how scared of me she was, I don't know if I'll ever forgive myself for making her hate me. She refused to even look my way the entire ride. I wanted to grab her by the chin and make her speak to me, but she's suffered enough rough treatment for a lifetime. Still, my heart cracked, knowing I'm the one who caused this. Marching back upstairs and demanding that she listen to me plays through my head, but the best thing for me to do is calm down. Right now, I could kill a motherfucker, and although I'd never physically hurt her, I'm not in the mood to be civil.

For now, I'm going to direct my anger where it belongs and deal with the asshole that had the nerve to steal my wife. I only knew of Cormack's brother from hushed whispers, and I had no idea how fucking nuts he really was.

I meet my men where they have Peter Delaney located.

I know Cormack isn't involved because he adores his wife like I worship Aria, and he's made it clear that he doesn't care for his brother Peter at all because he knows he's a piece of shit. It was a pure shock to see that Peter stole her from me. I can't wash that image from my head of her relaxing like she was going on vacation. If I hadn't seen Aria pop him on the head, I would have sworn she was content with being with him. I have to believe that she was playing it cool so he wouldn't snap and kill her.

I'm just about to hop into my vehicle when Cormack steps out of the shadows. My gun is ready along with three of my men who take my left and right, and he raises up his hands in a motion of truce. I never had a problem with Cormack before, but I will not hesitate to kill him if he tries to stop me from handling his piece-of-shit brother. "I'm going with you," he says. There's no way in hell he came to tell me to grant him mercy.

I wave my men to stand down. "Delaney, I'm not going to spare his life. He stole my wife. You're wasting your breath and my time."

"Don't worry. I'm not going to say it. I want him dead as much as you do. Blood or not, he's crossed the line in more than ways than I can count. I should have done it years ago but keeping him from Gloria and our family has been my only goal. I believe he killed his wife and my father."

"I'll get you those answers, but after that he won't be departing this building with a pulse." Or body parts intact, if I have my way.

"I want to be the one to kill him." I look at him and see that there's a vehemence. "I failed Aria too. I had seen his attraction to her years ago, but I thought he'd moved on. The last time he mentioned her name it wasn't sexual or with interest."

"He played it cool, but Aria's my wife and I should have

made sure she was protected, and I let those fucks into my home."

"How about we do this together?"

"That I can agree with." We shake hands and he joins me in my vehicle. All my thoughts should be on what I'm going to do to the asshole tied up, but in reality, they're on my wife. I want Aria to love me the way I love her, but I killed any chance of that. We make it to the warehouse that's been abandoned for twenty years, or at least so authorities and realtors believe.

Nero waits for us at the entrance of my special little meeting place. "Is Aria okay?"

"She's not physically hurt." I don't need to say anymore because the look on my face is enough.

"Understood." A muffled shout comes from inside. "He's still kicking and screaming, but I'm guessing his tone is going to change when he sees you two."

"I'm going to go in first and have him talk. Then you can get your vengeance, Delaney. We'll see how tough the fucker is now." I open the door and breathe in the room that once smelled like cleaner to take in the beautiful stench of piss. I love it when I know my enemies understand their fate and wet themselves like little bitches.

"Peter Delaney, is it?" I take in this fool's appearance. His already pale ass looks like a ghost. My guys bandaged him up enough so he wouldn't bleed out. It's only temporary, though, because he's not going to live long.

"Don't speak my name, you fucking wop." I brush off the insult with a chuckle because this guy is either crazy or foolish. He's on the wrong end of this situation.

"You called me a fucking wop. You've got some brass balls on you, Delaney. You send your minions into my home, put your filthy hands on my wife, and then attempt to take my place."

"She was never meant for you." His eyes darken with serious rage, and I realize he honestly thinks his words are going to scare me.

I laugh, because this fucking fool believes he deserves my Aria.

"I might not be good enough for her, but she was meant for me and not someone who kills off his own family. First your father, and then your own wife—how the fuck do you sleep at night?"

"Just fine. They had to go. Besides, it's Aria who would give me the family I deserve. Siobhan was never good enough for me, and that baby wasn't good enough to be a Delaney." Wow, this fucker killed his pregnant wife.

"You should have stuck with the bride you had. Now you've signed your death warrant."

"You're going to kill me because you're afraid that your wife truly does want me. You had to keep her hidden so she couldn't find a man on her own." It's the same words that she tossed at me which strikes a nerve.

"Did your operative lie and tell her that? I protected her from an abduction, and I let my guard down, Delaney. That won't happen again." I punch the bastard in the face, causing his head to toss back.

"Pussy," he spits out, blood dripping down his face.

"You are a fool, Peter," Cormack says, coming out of the darkness and up to his brother. There's a pain in his eyes that he quickly masks. "You murdered a great woman. I had no proof, but I knew you had a hand in your wife's death. Why did you kill our father?"

"He was about to give it all to you, disown me and make you the head of the Delaney Family. He paid the price of betraying me." Sick motherfucker. "If he'd done that I would have killed you both. You should be grateful I spared you. And this is what you to do me. Betray me for this wop. He stole Aria from me and you know it."

"Aria has always been repulsed by you, and for good reason. Say your prayers for forgiveness."

"Fuck off." Cormack pulls the trigger without giving him another thought. I take the gun from my brother-in-law. Cormack says a quick prayer and walks out of the building without a glance back.

I have everything I need, and he's no longer a threat to Aria.

"Get rid of this scum," I add to my men, giving the dead bastard one more glare before

"Go take care of your wife. You can fix it," Nero says. I clap his shoulder and nod before leaving. Going to see Aria after everything between us will be difficult. Still, she's my wife, and we'll have to make it work out, even if it takes time. I've learned to be patient when it comes to waiting for her, so I'll just have to try again until she understands that everything I had a part in was only for her own well-being.

As soon as I'm in my truck, I feel a sense of relief even though I should have been the one to take him out. Cormack had even more reasons which is fucking sick because I could never imagine killing my father. I look at him as he sits in silence. "I'm sorry you had to do that."

"It was a long time coming. I just need to see Gloria now."

"Let's get our women." The drive home goes by fast for me, but Cormack doesn't say another word. I can't even fathom what he's going through right now. I could never hurt Niccolò let alone kill him. Then again, my brother isn't a sick, twisted bastard.

I get home and climb the stairs, my body feeling sluggish. Ignoring the few guards in my house, I make my way to our bedroom door. Opening it slowly, I find the bed empty. I practically throw the door open, only to find my wife sleeping on the window seat, dressed in just her bathrobe. As I approach, I see the stains of the tears she shed from the weight of the last day.

Damn, it destroys me to see her like that. If it wasn't for the tears, she'd look like a goddess sleeping there, similar to her painting where she waits for her lover.

Scooping her up in my arms, I carry her to our bed. Slowly she adjusts in my arms and sighs my name. "Domani." She snuggles into my chest, and I feel for a brief moment that there's a chance she'll forgive me.

I regrettably set her down onto the mattress so that I can undress. She turns slightly, waking up just enough to notice I'm home. "You're home. What time is it?" She sits up against the headboard, rubbing her eyes to wake completely up.

"It's only been a couple of hours. Nearly two in the morning."

"Thank you for rescuing me."

"Don't thank me for doing what shouldn't have been necessary."

"I'm sorry."

"For what?"

"For everything I said. I shouldn't have said those things to you. My father's the one who kept me sheltered, even if it was to stop a war, but from what Peter said, it's clear you two were only trying to protect me from being abducted."

"Well, we didn't do a good job because he got to you anyway."

"Yes, but you were able to save me."

"Just barely."

"How were you able to find me?"

I rub my hand over the back of my neck. "Your ring. I made sure to attach a tracker in there."

"Were you afraid I'd run away?"

"No. I was worried someone would steal you from me. You're the most important person to me, my biggest weakness. From the first moment I made it known, I'd made you a target. Although when it came to that asshole, I thought he had no interest in you when questioned years ago."

"You questioned people?"

"It was when the attempted abduction almost occurred. What they didn't know is that I was so obsessed, I was stalking you every chance I got. You were on your way to school when I saw the bastard trying to swipe you up and my men apprehended him. He refused to tell us who hired him, but he had a southern accent, so our men went on the search. After that, no movement was made, so we concluded that he'd been working alone. We also uncovered that he was a serial killer, targeting young, beautiful women from sixteen to twenty."

"Oh my goodness, so if you hadn't been following me..."

"I don't know if he would have been successful, but that was a chance your family and I didn't really want to take. I'm sorry that we didn't tell you—give you a choice."

"Don't be. When I think about it, I'm glad you both did what you did. I would have lived in fear, looking over my shoulder if you'd told me the truth. Knowing that he was a serial killer makes it worse, but Peter said that he tried to abduct me and he missed his opportunity."

"Maybe you had two animals on you, but he hadn't made his move before we stopped the other one. For years, I know I blamed myself for putting a target on your back, but I knew if I didn't make my moves, then I'd be going to war with the other families. Your father promised I could marry you if I promised to not make contact with you until you were of legal age, so I did."

"For real?"

"Amore, I'm a criminal, just like him. Laws don't mean much to me, but respect does. Your father wanted me to prove my loyalty to you without trying to influence your choice."

"Wow, so you've been in love with me for years?"

"Yes, amore. I've loved you from the first moment you crossed my path."

"There's something I must confess. I've been thinking about you even longer. I was thirteen when I got my first look at you. You were with your cousin. I wasn't sure where you were going, but our vehicle and yours were at a light. You couldn't see me behind the tints, but I saw you. I'd been looking for images of you for years on the internet. Then, when you were in the meeting two years ago, I felt a change. It wasn't just a crush anymore. I hoped that you wouldn't marry by the time I'd grown up."

"You have, amore?"

"Yes. I love you very much. Why do you think I didn't put up much of a fight? I wanted to be your wife, but I loved the gruff, sexy way you reminded me I was yours."

"Wife, don't tease me right now. You've had a rough day, and I'm too worked up. I'll end up fucking you to the mattress all night long."

"I need you, Domani. I need a reminder that we're meant to be together." I'm on her, giving her purchase as I claim her mouth in a fierce kiss that I've been waiting for all day. I pull off just enough to let her breathe, skimming my lips along her face, creeping down her neck and back up.

"Domani," she sighs. The sound hits my soul, deeply calling to every part of me. I slip my fingers into her hair, tugging her head back so that I can lick her neck.

"Who do you belong to, Aria?"

"You. You are the only person I've ever wanted."

"Good." I tug on her tie, opening her robe. Her nipples stiffen as I graze the soft cotton across her pebbled skin. My eyes linger over her body—perfect, gorgeous, and all just for me. "These are all mine," I breathe out, sliding my tongue over her sexy breasts, sucking on her plump curves. Soon they'll be full of milk to feed our sons. She shivers as I swipe along her hard nipples. I bite down lightly so I can hear her moans. Every sound is breathy, need shooting from her lips. I slide one hand over her soft skin and along her silky curls, only stopping when my fingers find their target. Pumping one finger into her soaked core, I love how wet she is. "Do you want to come for me? Only me?"

"Always you. Only you." I pull my fingers from her cunt and slip them into my mouth without taking my eyes from her. "You taste so good, but I have to be in you or I'll lose my mind."

"Take me. I need to feel you deep inside. Please Domani."

"You never have to beg." I stand and strip out of my clothes as fast as humanly possible and then position myself at her entrance. With another deep kiss, I slam inside of her tight hole, claiming my wife all over again. She's gonna need —better yet, I'm gonna need—to be reminded daily that she belongs to me.

Running my hands up and down her soft, smooth skin, I bend my head breathe in the smell of my wife, loving the way her body begins to heat up. "You're mine, Aria. You have always been mine."

"I have and will always be yours," she says, tugging her hands through my hair and bringing my face to hers for a deep, soul penetrating kiss. I lift one leg up, wrapping it around my waist as I turn her slightly on an angle, driving into her intensifying my thrusts with every whimper and moan.

"Fuck, Dom, I'm coming," she screams out and I let go as well, jetting my load into her womb.

I flip us around so that she's resting on top of me. Brushing her hair out of her face, I kiss her lips and say, "I love you so much, Aria."

"My love for you has been years in the making, Domani." She tells me about the day they headed to the wedding. Had I known, I would have gone with her and then fucking killed Peter a long time ago with my bare hands.

We roll around as I piston in and out of her, fucking all night long, coming repeatedly until we're unable to move.

EPILOGUE

Domani

"WHAT THE FUCK do you mean you have a witness? Get rid of them," I shout at Nero as if he's not aware of how we operate.

"I thought we didn't hurt innocents?" Nero never even bothers to ask questions; something has to be up.

He's in the middle of a shitty subdivision in the southwest suburbs. The area has gone from an expensive neighborhood to a fucking cesspool in a matter of a decade. "Since when is there an innocent in that area?"

"She's a sales rep from a solar company." A she. Fuck, that's even worse. If it was some asshole that I could tempt or scare into keeping quiet, that would be better, but an innocent woman is another story all together.

"Solar company?" I tap my pen on my desk, wondering who would go into that area to install solar panels. That shit better be insured because it'll be plucked off of roofs and sold in a heartbeat to another company.

"Yeah, authentic and everything. She's going door-to-door and shit, like it's fucking safe," he snarls as if he's pissed about her type of employment. Is there more to this?

"Damn it. What's really going on, Nero? I get you don't want to hurt her, but we can't do nothing."

"We can't hurt her," he roars, making me laugh. Yep. My guy, my second-in-command, has the same problem I had: falling for a woman he couldn't have. "Wait, Dom. I have a plan, but you're not going to like it."

"What is it?"

"I'm going to keep her hostage and change her mind."

"What?" I play along, but I can read his tone of voice and know all I need to know.

"Let's just say I can't hurt her."

"This is on you, Nero," I remind him because I'm still the boss, and if this goes south, we could all be fucked.

"Domani, where are you?" Aria calls out, sounding fucking annoyed, which means I'm in trouble for something even though I haven't done shit to earn her ire.

"I've got to go; the queen is summoning me."

"Okay. I'll talk to you later." Humor returns to his voice, and I end the call.

"Domani, there you are," Aria huffs, coming into the room with our baby boy on her arm.

I'm up on my feet and around my desk in a flash. "What's wrong?"

She grins from ear to ear and squeals, "He said his first word." God, she's beautiful. I live for that smile.

"What?" I ask my little man who is also my pride and joy. We had to wait a couple of months before Aria became pregnant with Luca. I anxiously waited every month, but the damn period came anyway. He was my Christmas present though. Aria surprised me Christmas morning with the news that I was going to be a papa.

"Yes."

"What did he say?"

"Papa." My eyes fly open because I expected him to say "mama" or "baba" or something else. We spend a lot of time with him, but I'm dealing with business matters most of the day, both the legal and illegal side, so he doesn't see me anywhere near as much as he does Aria.

"Say it again for your papa," I coo, grabbing his chubby little fingers.

"Pa-pa. Pa-pa." A little drool dribbles out of his mouth, so I pull out my handkerchief and wipe it away. One day he'll rule all of this, but for now, he's my little bambino, my pride and joy who needs me to care for him the way a father should.

"Good boy!" I take him from his beautiful mama and kiss his head, which is covered in jet black hair. He takes after both of us so much, although everyone says he's gonna look just like me—but I don't mind if he looks like his mama. Either way, the little man is going to be a heartbreaker.

"He's learning quickly. According to the books, he's ahead of schedule," Aria cheers, clapping her hands softly. Luca grabs her hands and claps them for her. He's an intelligent baby for sure.

"He's going to be a smart little one like his uncle Niccolò." Aria and I are above average, but my brother's a genius and a nerd, so I wouldn't mind at all if he took after him.

"Speaking of, Niccolò. He's been taking some time off lately."

"What do you mean?"

"Well, your mom and I went to go get some coffee this

morning at the one café in town that we love, and Niccolò was there."

"Yes, well, the owner owes us a pretty penny. I have Nico checking out the financial stability of the place."

"Si, but that's not what he's doing. He's watching the girl behind the counter. I don't know if it's his first time being there or if he's been going there, but he was watching her like the way you watch me."

"What? He's falling too?"

"I don't know, but I think it's possible. He's got that Domani look that says, 'Mine.'"

"You mean this one?"

"Mm-hmm," she sighs as I press my lips to hers.

"That's because us Bianchi men know what's ours and claim it."

"Whoa, whoa. Where do you think you're going, buddy?" He's getting stronger and searching for independence every day. At eight months, he's already standing up against surfaces. It won't be long until he's walking.

"He's ready to run, Domani. Aren't you, Luca?"

"He's gonna be just like me. We're in for it, for sure. I used to run up and down these halls until I cracked my head open—right here." I point to a faint scar in my hairline.

"Let's hope he doesn't have any major accidents. I don't think my heart could take it." Luca stretches out his hands for Mama, tugging away from me. I hand him back so he doesn't fall because he's too damned stubborn like his daddy.

"So do you want to come out to the pool with us?"

"Yes, my queen. I could use some time with my little family. Besides, I believe you said you had a new bikini for me to see."

"Maybe I should wait to wear it. I've gotten a little heavier lately."

"Are we going to have this discussion again? I think you are sexy, even if you put on another hundred pounds."

"Hardly, but I mean... well, I suppose if I don't wear it now, I might never get a chance with you putting babies in me."

"Babies? Amore, are you pregnant?"

"Surprise?"

"Yes. Hell, yes, Aria," I growl, sliding my hand into her hair and pulling her close to me. Our boy pats my face, but I need to kiss my wife so I take him out of her arms and set him down in the play yard I have in my office. I might be a mob boss, but my kids mean the world to me—every single one we're blessed with. Dragging Aria to me, I press her body to mine as I taste her soft lips. "Forget swimming; I need to get you alone."

"Well, then, I guess it's good that I asked your mom to watch Luca for the afternoon. All we have to do is drop him off in her wing."

"I'm on it," I growl, scooping up my little guy and hearing Aria's laughter give way as I march out of my office to my parents' part of the house. Although we share the majority of it, they do have a private bedroom for the grandkids to come. Luca's the first of many on my side of the family. Gloria and Delaney have gone about it the good ol' Irish Catholic way, and they're on baby number four. We won't be far behind if I get my way.

Right now, they're in Ireland so that Delaney can handle matters over there because his brother ran their name to shit. I still regret killing Peter so quickly, but I can rejoice that he no longer walks the earth, and it will be the same for whoever tries to harm my family, because they mean everything to me.

"Wow, I thought you would have gotten here faster," my mother teases.

"I was reveling in the fact that my little man said my name. Now here he is. You need anything, send me a text, but I think Aria could use some time to celebrate."

"Enjoy. Say bye-bye to Papa and Mama."

"Bye," he coos. Aria spins around and I follow suit, giving my Luca another kiss. It takes us another ten minutes to pull away from him, even though we're ready for an evening to ourselves.

"So, did you arrange this today?"

"Nope. I just mentioned that I was tired, and your mama demanded that I bring Luca for the night."

"Are you tired?"

"My arms are tired, but I love holding him."

"He's gonna be too heavy for you to be carrying soon. When do you see the doctor?"

"Tomorrow, and then she can tell me what I should and shouldn't be doing," she says, glaring at me with that attitude that's going to get her fucked nice and hard.

"Are you getting smart with me, wife?"

"I've always had a smart mouth. I've just been a really good girl lately." Her eyes dart upward as she purses her lips sweetly.

"Little liar."

She presses her hand to her chest. "Who, me? I'm an angel."

"You're the devil's angel, and I'll take the good, the bad, and the dirty any time, amore. Now, get on your knees and make up for that mouth of yours." She smiles up at me, knowing damned well that's exactly what she wants. Aria gets horny as hell when pregnant, and thank fuck for that.

Kneeling, she takes my cock out and slips it into her warm mouth. "Fuck," I hum. The way she takes her times, dragging her tongue under my shaft and back up, swallowing around my head almost breaks me. The slow pace intensifies my orgasm, and my wife knows it. She wants to drive me insane and then let me nut down her slender throat.

The vibrations coming from her cause me to groan and I press my fingers around her neck, squeezing just enough for her to spread her thighs and reach for her pussy which I'm sure is ready to coat our wood floors.

I tug on her hair and look down at my gorgeous wife. "Are you getting ready to cream?"

"Yes," she purrs around my cock. As much as I want to come, I need to feel her walls clench around me as I cum. I reluctantly pull out. "No," she says, pouting.

"I need to feel you. I'm going to fuck you long and hard while you take your pleasure, wife." Scooping her up, I lay my queen on our bed, parting her thighs and kissing her reddened knees before sliding my tongue through her puffy pink slit.

"Fuck me, my king." I do.

"Forever, my queen." I slam into her heat, taking Aria hard over and over until she shakes, moans, and arches her back while her pussy spasms around my length which always sends me with her. If she wasn't already carrying my baby, she'd be pregnant again.

I'll never get enough of Aria.

EPILOGUE

Aria

Ten years later

FIVE KIDS, and we have the sixth on the way. When Domani said he wanted to outdo my sister and her husband, I didn't take him seriously. The man would happily put another ten in me if he could. I'm sure he could, but I'm not going to let him.

"How's my beautiful wife?"

"You mean your Bianchi factory?" I huff, feeling fat. I've been blessed to lose all the baby fat with each kid, but I always get as round as a house when I'm pregnant. Tears well up in my eyes before they break free, coming down my face.

"Baby, stop crying. You're killing me. I can't take your tears," Domani begs. I love the sounds of his voice, but right now all I can think about is how men cheat on their pregnant wives, so it's only a matter of time before Domani does the same.

"I'm a whale. You're going to find someone else."

"Whoa, wife. I'm about to forget you're about to go into labor and bend you over the bed to spank your ass. I love you, and I'm not going anywhere. I'm gonna die before you, and I'm still gonna be lingering until we meet again. What's going on? Who made you think like that?"

"I was watching Maury...." I sob.

He throws his hands up in the air with a huff before pulling me into his arms. "Lord help me. Amore, from now on, only happy shows. Fucking videos of puppies and kittens doing silly shit. This little girl is causing so much emotion."

"I'm sorry, Domani. I don't mean to be a pain," I cry, turning away from him.

"Aria Bianchi, turn your ass around right now and look at me," he growls, using that voice that turns me on. Suddenly my tears dry up. "Listen to me, and listen good. You can cry, but the second the six weeks are up, I'm gonna punish you for doubting my love and devotion. I'm going to eat you out over and over, bringing you to the brink of coming and then do it all over until you understand that you're mine and will always be mine. I don't want anyone else. Are we clear?" he asks, running his hands over my breasts, stiffening my nipples.

"Yes," I stutter out a moan.

"Good, cara mia. Now let's wash your face and join the family down for dinner. You're going to eat your food and forget any ideas of you being too big for me. You're my queen, and I am your king. We're in this forever."

"But I'm not hungry."

"You know I don't like to repeat myself."

"I'll eat." I don't get these rollercoaster emotions. I'm a freaking basket case. I need to find sweet stuff to watch or read, but I still cry because it's just so beautiful. "Oh no."

"What's going on?"

"I don't think I can eat." I freeze then and groan as pain shoots through my stomach and back. Domani's strong arms wrap around me, and I'm off my feet and cradled all the way down the stairs.

He turns to Marco, one of his guards, and says, "Code Pink."

The front doors are opened a minute later, and his SUV with Luigi driving is brought up front. The guards open the door and Domani slides me inside. Through the break between contractions, I put it together that Domani put a plan in place for when I went into labor. He's never done it with the boys before.

"What's with the code PINK?" I growl out through the next contraction.

"My little princess is coming. I wanted to make sure we were prepared for her."

"So then there's an ivory tower ready?"

"Not yet. She's not going to leave the house until she's at least six and my crew can construct it in less than six months." I'd laugh, but I'm not sure he's joking. From the look on his face, I don't believe he is. I laugh anyway because he's insane and knowing my past, I might be on board with the plan when the time comes.

"At least we'll let her know why she's locked in her gilded cage."

"I'm glad you see things my way." He winks at me and then kisses my temple. "I was only kidding, my queen. I can't say I won't be protective of her, but I'll just make sure she has more security than the President of the United States."

"That works for me. Ouch," I scream the last bit as another pain shoots through my back to my pussy..

"We better hurry. Someone is impatient."

We barely make it to the entrance and are covered in sweat when my water breaks. I'm quickly wheeled into the hospital, where I give birth to our daughter, Mia Carina. She's a big girl at ten pounds and twenty-three inches long. As I wake up from my nap, I take in the sight before me. My Mia rests on her papa's bare chest like a total princess with a bow and all. He's quietly singing to her as she sleeps. It's the most beautiful thing to see.

I'll be forever grateful that I was married to the mob.

ABOUT THE AUTHOR

C.M. Steele is a bestselling author on Amazon with over 120 books to read and enjoy!

C.M. Steele's Book List:
Best Friends Series:
Always You
His Dirty Secret
Sleep Tight
A Best Friends Duet:
Picture Perfect
Instant Obsession
The Captive Series:
Luciano's Willing Captive
The Russian's Captive
Sergei's Stubborn Captive
The Caught Series:
Caught In A Case
Caught Off Guard
Caught in A Lie
Caught Crossing the Line
Caught Breaking the Law
Caught Red Handed
Cavanaugh Security Series:
Protecting Macy
Securing Blake
The Cline Brothers of Colorado:
Whatever it Takes

Taking Whatever he Wants
Finding Paradise
Dark Hearts Series:
Intense
The Falling Series:
Falling for the Boss
Falling for the Enemy
Falling Hard
Family & Friends:
Wanting it All
Chasing his Sunshine
Lassoing His Cowgirl
Ben's Resolve
Gimme Series:
Sugar
Luck
Rain
Cream
Heat
The James Family:
No Choice
No Way Out
No More Waiting
The Kane Family:
His Christmas Rose
Her Christmas Surprise
His Candy Kane
Christmas in July
Keepsakes:
Keeping Blossom
Keep in Mind
The Lamian Wars:
Bound

Reveal

Release

All Hallows Eve

Love Bites Series:

Love Bites

Once Bitten

The Middleton Hotels:

Built for Me

Built to Last

Built Strong

Built Over Time

Built Overnight

Nothing but Trouble Series:

Taking the Bait

Taking the Mafia Princess

The O'Connell Family:

Claiming Red

Burning for Claire

Claiming Abby

Reminding Red

Obsessed Alpha Series:

Stone

Cole

Graham

Theo

Maddox

Alessandro

Tony

A Rough Hands Novella:

My Miracle

Nailing my Wife

Say Something Series:

Say Uncle

Down South

Gone South

Sweetheart's Treats:

Sweet Surprise

Doctor's Orders, Sweetheart

Sweet Surrender

Twin Sin:

Stalk Me Please

Sinful Intent

White Wolf Ridge Series:

Turner

Wolfe Creek Series:

Wolfe's Den

Beta: Her Alpha

Raging Kane

Written in History

Others:

Buying Love

Christmas in Camden

Conquering Alexandria

Grant's Deal

Hunting Allegra

Killer Abs

Love Discovered

Loving My Neighbor

Mrs. Valentine

My Christmas Gift

Rainy Days Stormy Nights

Red Hot Nights

Room Service

Scarred

Sharp Curves

So Wrong

Standing There
Stealing Beauty
Taking the Thief
The Wedding Guest
Unexpected

www.ingramcontent.com/pod-product-compliance
Lightning Source LLC
Chambersburg PA
CBHW071928220626
47052CB00002B/499

* 9 7 8 1 9 5 4 6 4 5 0 6 6 *